MIDLOTHIAN LIBRARY SERVICE

Please return/renew this item by the last date shown. To renew please give your borrower number. Renewal may be made in person, online, or by post, e-mail or phone.
www.midlothian.gov.uk/library

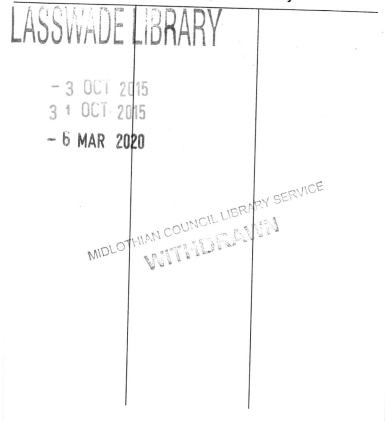

THE illmoor
CHRONICLES
The Dwellings Debacle

More Illmoor Chronicles from David Lee Stone

The Ratastrophe Catastrophe
The Yowler Foul-up
The Shadewell Shenanigans

THE illmoor
CHRONICLES

The Dwellings Debacle

DAVID LEE STONE

Hodder
Children's
Books

A division of Hodder Headline Limited

A Catalogue record for this book is available
from the British Library

ISBN 0 340 89368 0

Typeset in NewBaskerville by Avon DataSet Ltd,
Bidford-on-Avon, Warwickshire

Printed and bound in Great Britain by
Clays Ltd, St Ives plc

The paper and board used in this paperback by
Hodder Children's Books are natural recyclable products
made from wood grown in sustainable forests.
The manufacturing processes conform to the environmental
regulations of the country of origin.

Hodder Children's Books
a division of Hodder Headline Limited
338 Euston Road
London NW1 3BH

This book is for my uncle, John 'Mick' Ford,
who would undoubtedly be a friend of Groan Teethgrit
if he lived in Illmoor. It's also for Teresa,
Maria and Peter.

Selected Dramatis Personae
(ye cast of characters)

Burnie	– Troglodyte councillor.
Curfew, Contessa	– Wife of the viscount.
Curfew, Ravis	– Viscount; Lord of Dullitch.
Daily, Parsnip	– A tracker.
Diveal, Sorrell	– A noble.
Dwellings, Enoch	– A detective.
Innesell	– A prisoner.
LaVale, Tikki	– A Guard Marshal.
Mardris, Lusa	– A detective's assistant.
Morkus, Private	– A guard.
Obegarde, Jareth	– A loftwing detective.
Quickstint, Jimmy	– A gravedigger.
Spires, Milquay	– Royal secretary.
Stoater	– A matchstick man.
Wheredad, Doctor	– An assistant detective.

. . . and others.

ILLMOOR

GRINSWOOD FOREST

LEGRASH

BEANSTALK

CHUDDERFORD

SNEEZE

RIVER WASHOUT

LITTLE IRKESOME

SHINBONE

SHINBONE
FOREST

SHADEWELL

CRUST

GLEAMING MOUNTAINS

CARAEAT JUNGLES

DULLITCH

Prologue

'I don't like this,' the traveller whispered to his friend. 'I don't like this *at all*.'

Having been caught short of common sense in the wilderness north of Crust, they'd been delighted to discover a dilapidated coaching inn amid the fierce woodlands. However, their delight had soon changed to dubious apprehension when the place turned out to be full of strangely inhospitable locals. They could forgive the sniggering dwarves at the corner table and the odd looks from the group of farmers huddled beside the bar, but there was something seriously *amiss* with the hooded man sitting next to the fire, cracking his jaw, and the innkeeper with the black moustache (who they strongly suspected was two teeth short of a beaver). Worse still, there was now a silent yet unsubtle exchange running between the innkeeper and his fireside customer, albeit from far ends of the room.

'I bet it's about us,' said the first traveller, licking his trembling lips. 'Did you see that bit where he walked his two fingers along the bar top? That might be code for "hitchhikers" . . .'

The second traveller rolled his eyes.

'Oh, don't be so paranoid,' he said, smiling nervously.

'I'm not being paranoid – why aren't they just speaking to each other, like normal folk?'

'Perhaps they don't want the farmers listening in.'

'Ha! I doubt that. Look: the bloke beside the fire just ran a finger under his jaw – 'sa death signal, that! I just knew it was a bad idea to come in here! I mean; what kind of place is open at nearly *three o'clock in the morning* . . . ?'

'Go, then!'

'Aren't you coming?'

'Nope: I'm far too tired to go on, just now.'

Time passed. One by one, the farmers began to drink up and head out into the darkness. They were followed by the dwarves, who were all the worse for drink. Eventually, the inn became quiet, with only a crackle from the fireplace to hold back the silence.

'Let's get out of here; *please*,' whispered the first traveller, anxiety creeping into his voice.

'And go where? There probably isn't another inn for miles, at least not one that's open! Besides, we haven't even finished our drinks . . .'

The traveller stared down at the tankards.

'I don't like this ale, anyway,' he muttered. 'It tastes funny. I tell you, this place is knee-deep in the bad stuff . . .'

The man beside the fireplace abruptly folded his arms, then seemed to change his mind, and reached up to caress his jutting jaw.

The first traveller leaned close to his friend.

'You're not telling me *he's* balanced,' he whispered.

'Why, just because he's not running over here to engage us in conversation?'

'*No*, because he's wearing a hood and playing with his jawbone: that's *proper* mental.'

His friend gave a dispassionate shrug.

'Look, I'm cold, I'm hungry, and I'll be damned if I'm walking through the woods for another six miles. I'm staying here and that's that!'

'Fine,' snapped the traveller, snatching up his backpack and clambering to his feet. 'Well, just so you know, the innkeeper has dried blood all down the back of his coat: I saw it as I ordered the drinks . . .'

The traveller slung on his pack, and departed. When the door had slammed behind him, his friend made a disgruntled face and took another large swig of ale: it *did* taste funny, he had to admit.

The clock struck three. As the last of its chimes sounded throughout, the door of the inn creaked open, and a thin, spindly man with bulbous eyes and a strangely active tongue sidled his way in.

'We've got *it*, massster,' he spat, apparently addressing the hooded man. '*It'sssss* in the yard.'

That said, he hurried outside again.

The traveller looked on in a not-looking-on sort of way as the stranger beside the fire got carefully to his feet and followed.

'Open up the back,' the stranger called, as he passed the table. 'I'll give them a hand.'

'Right you are,' the innkeeper shouted after him, stomping off into the dark recesses of the inn.

Then, there was silence.

As the room's enormous fire crackled away, the traveller – now totally alone in the bar – began to feel very uncomfortable.

'Maybe it's an ale delivery or something,' he said to himself, but aloud, so the room didn't seem quite so menacing. 'Yeah, that'll be it: an ale delivery.'

Then it happened: a terrible scream, a cry of pain that pierced the silence of the inn and nearly caused the traveller to bite clean through his tongue. He jumped to his feet.

'What the hell was that?' he gasped, glancing around at the empty room. There was *still* no sign of the innkeeper.

He quickly snatched up his backpack, left an overly generous tip on the table and made his way to the door, but he hadn't gone more than ten steps when a deep, booming voice said:

'And where do you think *you're* going?'

The innkeeper had appeared at the bar, his spindly associate standing beside him.

'I – er – thought I might head off . . .' the traveller said with a forced smile, sweat beginning to bead on his brow.

'Oh, you did, did you?'

'Er . . . yes: I'm afraid so. It's getting late. Goodnight!'

There was a 'click' from behind him, and the traveller spun around: the hooded stranger from the fireplace had re-entered the inn and was lowering a bar across the door.

'Wh-what are you doing? What is this?'

He made to step around the man, then thought better of it and turned back to the innkeeper.

'What's going on here?'

The innkeeper smiled, displaying a grim formation of broken teeth, but neither he nor his snake-like companion spoke a word.

'LET – ME – OUT!' said the traveller, gritting his teeth, partly to show some mustard but mainly because it stopped his jaw from shaking. 'I'm going home, do you hear me? I don't belong here!'

'Oh, we know that,' whispered the hooded man,

putting a hand on the traveller's shoulder. 'But tonight, for us, is a very important night, when something we've planned for a very long time has come to pass.'

'W-what's that got to do with me?'

'Nothing. It's got nothing *at all* to do with you, but when your friend left earlier, he did so at a very inopportune moment . . . and he saw someone that he shouldn't have seen. He was in the *wrong* place at the *worst* possible time . . . as are you.'

The traveller's eyes filled with tears, and his lips began to tremble.

'B-but I'm not g-going to tell anyone . . .'

'Not good enough. Besides,' the stranger said, removing his hood. 'You've seen my face.'

The traveller stepped back, his jaw dropping. 'B-b-but I don't understand: aren't you Vi—'

There was a sudden, sickening *thud* and then . . . there was silence.

Part One

Problems at the Palace ...

One

Night . . . and down came the rain.

Guard Marshal Tikki LaVale didn't think much of Dullitch's wall-top sentries, not because he had particularly high standards or was in any way difficult to please, but simply because the sentries in Dullitch were *that* bad. Consequently, when a shadow appeared on the rooftops of the city's eastside, moving at an impossibly high speed and leaping chimney stacks as if they were pebbles, Tikki immediately determined to give chase himself.

Saying nothing to his lazy subordinates on the eight o'clock shift, he backed slowly away from the window, walked casually out of his office, climbed carefully down the rickety ladder that separated his own sentry box from those on the lower level, sneaked out of view along the dark alleyways opposite the city wall and promptly hared off across town like a crossbow bolt.

Tikki could run *fast* – he'd been able to ever since he was a boy – and he could also hurdle, so nothing short of an unexpected high wall was going to slow his progress. There were certainly no unexpected high walls in *this* part of Dullitch, where the houses were so close together that their upper storeys were affectionately known as 'kissers'.

Tikki dashed up the ridiculously narrow, uneven cobbled lanes until he found a house with something that thieves would have referred to as the 'golden drainpipe'. Spotting the property out of the corner of his eye, he hurried over to it, shinned up the pipe, scrambled on to the ramshackle roof and produced an old but very trusty spyglass from the depths of his jerkin.

The rooftop view appeared, and was quickly twisted into focus. It took Tikki a moment to find the shadow – mainly because the rain was lashing his face – but once he'd spotted it, he immediately knew from the divergence of direction and the incredible urgency of pace that it could only be heading for one location: the palace.

Tikki took a deep breath, and put on a burst of speed that he usually reserved for downing ale in the Ferret at closing time. In just under ten seconds, he'd crossed six roofs and made a very unlikely-looking jump between two buildings loosely linking the rich and poor districts. Recovering quickly, he dropped on to the dodgy slates of Finlayzzon's and, unfurling a coil of rope and a miniature grapple, managed to get halfway along the jutting buttresses of Karuim's Church before slipping in the unforgiving rain and sliding awkwardly to the street below.

No time for such a mistake . .

He groaned as he struggled up from the mud, then swung the rope around in a wild arc and began the frantic climb back to the top of the church. Progress was fast, but not nearly fast enough for Tikki's liking. Finally, engraved with grit, grime and countless scratches, he hauled himself on to the highest of the church's many spires, locked the grapple in place and lowered himself gently over the side.

Drawing level with the palace walls, he kicked himself away from the church's north face and landed squarely on the battlements opposite. His rope was more difficult to retrieve this time, so much so that he almost left it, but eventually perseverance paid off.

So . . . around the palace wall . . .

. . . through a door in the (alarmingly empty) guard post . . .

. . . and down the spiral staircase.

Then outside, across the palace gardens . . .

. . . grappling iron ready . . .

... swing ...

... and up to the palace roof.

Tikki LaVale, through determination, speed and an outstanding knowledge of the city's myriad by-ways, arrived on the roof of Dullitch Palace, sparing just enough time to draw his sword as his target landed on the other side of the building's wide roof.

The shadow – for it was wreathed in a black, billowing cloak – rolled as it landed, depositing a small box on the rooftop, then leaped up and drew two swords with such speed that, for a moment, Tikki thought he might have imagined the move. Anticipating an immediate strike, he knelt and readied his own blade.

Then came a shock; as the figure drew near to the Guard Marshal, it pulled back the hood covering its face.

Relief flooded over Tikki LaVale.

'Human,' he said, gritting his teeth against the pelting rain. 'I'll admit I'm surprised; I thought at the very least you'd be Elfin. What's in the box? Doomchuck powder? An explosive of some kind? Oh no, I see it's moving. A poison lizard, then? Very original.'

The stranger paid no attention to Tikki's words. Instead, he darted forward, whirled the two blades in a complicated web and swiftly struck out with them.

Tikki blocked both shots with his own sword.

'Two things,' he said, squinting through the downpour. 'One: though I'm impressed with that turn of speed you showed in getting here, I should advise you that I was further away, and I still got here first. And two: it wouldn't be fair of me not to tell you that – with the possible exception of Viscount Curfew himself – I'm probably the best sword in the city, so don't even think—'

Tikki was interrupted by two immediate strikes, followed by a somersault and a third. Still, despite the fact that he parried all three, the action worried him enough to take a step back and study the face of his attacker.

'Who are you?' he said, gazing from the small, beady eyes to the straggly, rain-soaked hair. 'What do you want here?'

The two men circled each other, looking for an opening.

'I assume you're here for the viscount,' Tikki went on, while measuring the time between lightning strikes to see if it would aid his cause. 'Who sent you? Legrash? Phlegm? Spittle? Hmm . . . funny, somehow you don't look like an assassin . . .'

The fifth blow was aimed directly at Tikki's face, and he dodged it with comparative ease: perhaps the talk was helping.

'I say you don't look like an assassin because assassins are usually smart enough to keep themselves covered up,' he continued, smiling through a particularly vicious rumble of thunder. 'Then again, maybe you're just confident . . .'

Nothing was spoken by the stranger, but a sixth strike followed, then a seventh.

Tikki dived down to block the last blow, and realised with sudden, terrible horror that he'd left himself open to . . .

Ssssk.

Tikki grabbed for his throat, but he'd incorrectly predicted the stranger's move: the throat wound was merely a scratch to divert attention from . . .

'Argghh!'

He staggered back, the stranger's second sword buried deep in his chest, and . . .

. . . down came the rain.

The swordsman dragged the body of Tikki LaVale across the palace roof and deposited it beside one of the more magnificent buttresses. Then he retrieved the box he'd been carrying and crept carefully towards the upper stairwell hatch.

When he pulled on the brass ring and lifted the sturdy hatch, relief flooded over him: there were no guards on duty at the top of the tower. Ha! That would make the task *so* much easier than he had anticipated.

The swordsman slipped inside the tower and began to descend the spiral staircase: his box was shaking now, as the creature inside fought to escape its squat prison.

Down. Down. And out: into the main body of the palace.

The swordsman kept out of sight, expertly nipping between shade and shadow to ease his path through the draughty corridors.

At length, he arrived at Korvan's Kitchen: the very heart of Dullitch Palace. A plaque above the doorway reminded all of Korvan, the legendary and somewhat officious cook who served Lord Bowlcock, the first Duke of Dullitch.

The swordsman didn't bother to study the plaque, however, choosing instead to sneak around the edge of the kitchen, narrowly avoiding two stout servants that supported a giant soup-cauldron between them.

When the kitchen was blissfully empty, the swordsman made his move. Accepting that the solitude wouldn't last long, he swiftly tossed the box on to the nearest workbench, snapped off the catch and yanked open the lid. Then he snaked a hand into the silky depths of the inner case and pulled out a small, wriggling creature with a thick head of fur, three black eyes and a gleaming set of tiny, needle-sharp teeth.

The swordsman whistled at the creature, which abruptly ceased its struggling and began to mew like a contented kitten.

'Saving up that wonderful noise?' he whispered, and, reaching down with his other hand, he produced two wads of cotton wool from his robe.

As if sensing imminent danger, the creature began to

struggle again, clawing at the fist that held it aloft by its hair.

A tabby cat watched from a nearby bench as the swordsman jabbed a cotton-ball firmly into each ear, and drew a thin and extremely nasty-looking blade from his belt.

'The stage is all yours,' he said to his restless captive. Then he stabbed it vigorously in the stomach.

A few minutes later, the swordsman replaced the dead creature inside its box, and prepared to leave the kitchen. He stepped over a number of prone servants and several patches of shattered glass on his way to the first floor.

Two

Viscount Curfew looked up from his writing desk, his quill poised over the leather-bound diary that lay open upon it.

Another flash: how he *hated* lightning. Still, his fear of the electric wrath was as nothing to his fear of the noise that always followed it. Thankfully, he had his earplugs firmly wedged in, and the mirrors had all been turned to face the wall: safety, first.

The viscount stared out of the window opposite his desk at the rooftops of eastern Dullitch. It was a humid night, something that would undoubtedly help to prolong the storm.

Still, he was far too busy to worry about such

things: storm or no storm, he had work to do.

Curfew returned his attention to the diary, and was about to put quill to parchment, when there came a loud clatter from the direction of the stairs.

The viscount sighed, threw down his quill and stomped over to the bedroom door. However, because he was at all times a cautious man, he drew his sword before he opened it.

No assassin, then, he thought, casting an annoyed glance at the men in grimy overalls who were attempting to fold a white sheet at the top of the stairs. He noticed that, as usual, his room guards were both fast asleep.

'You two!' he snapped at the sheet-folders. 'What are you doing?'

The largest of the pair, a veritable *lion* of a man, turned to face him.

'Cleaners, guv: we're putting these sheets away.'

Curfew rolled his eyes.

'Well, try not to make so much noise.'

'Right you are. Sorry, guv.'

'Hmm,' Curfew began, a frown developing on his brow. 'They look weighed down in the middle: do you have someone wrapped up in there? You do, don't you?'

In answer to this, the big man heaved at one end of the sheet, and a bruised and battered body fell out.

Curfew started, and strained to see the face of the prone figure.

'Isn't that the fellow who delivers the vegetables?' he enquired.

'Dunno,' hissed the second sheet-folder, who was a good deal smaller than his companion. 'Isss it?'

'Yes! What happened to him?'

'He ssstuck his nose in where it wasn't wanted; gave usss some trouble while we were trying to scrub the floors.'

'He looks dead.'

'Nah,' growled the giant. 'He'll be all right with a jug of ale thrown over 'im.'

Viscount Curfew sighed.

'Fine; just keep the noise down, will you?' he snapped. Then he turned and shut the portal behind him. Unfortunately, in doing so he failed to notice that the ears of his snoring room sentries were bleeding.

Back in the bedchamber, Curfew muttered under his breath and carefully locked the oak door: then he turned round a second too late to avoid a gloved fist slamming into his face.

He fell back against the wall, shook his head and frantically brought up his sword, just as the assassin he'd been expecting to see in the corridor drew his own weapon.

Three

It was early morning in Dullitch, and the icy shades of the night before were just beginning to recede.

Down in the square, the first market traders were starting to assemble their stalls and several greedy merchants were preparing their caravans with great enthusiasm: it was all business as usual.

Up at the palace, however, things couldn't have been more different . . .

Milquay Spires, royal secretary to the ruling lord of Dullitch, awoke in a pool of his own blood, which was never a good sign . . .

He tried to lift his head, but it felt too heavy and he

20

triggered off an unbearable neck pain in the process.

What had happened? Why couldn't he remember anything?

'Help!' he shouted, but the sound came out muffled, as though he was talking through a mouthful of cotton wool. Moreover, his arms and legs were numb.

'Guards! GUARDS!' He was shouting now, booming at the top of his voice, yet it still felt like *whispering*, even in his head.

'P-please . . . somebody.'

Spires found, to his frustrated embarrassment, that he was crying. Tears formed in the corner of his eyes and saliva dripped from the edge of his mouth on to the carpet.

'Help.'

The secretary gave one last gasp before his vision faded, and he lost consciousness. Time passed . . .

. . . and nothing happened.

Eyelids flickered in the light.

'Is this the end? Am I dead?'

It took a few seconds for Spires to recognise that he was speaking *real* words, very clearly. He tried again, saying: 'Somebody help!'

Then he realised that he didn't need assistance.

Spires began to peer around him. His office was not only devoid of attackers; worse than that, it was entirely normal.

Still no memory . . .

. . . and still the blood.

The viscount's secretary jerked his neck around in order to look behind him, sharply feeling the pain he'd suffered previously.

His suspicions were immediately proved wrong: there was no one standing over him with a sword, no one rifling through his desk and no one climbing precariously out of the window. There was nothing, in fact, but heady silence.

Right, then . . .

Spires bit his lip as he pushed himself off the ground, partly because he was expecting some sort of surprise offensive but *mostly* because he was sure that several of his bones were broken. It would have surprised him to know that neither was the case.

Attaining his stance, the secretary took a deep breath and tried to think. The first word he thought of was 'theft', and, being a man devoutly respectful of his gut instincts, he gritted his teeth and started to look around.

When a cursory search of the room turned up nothing, he limped across to the office's grand wall-mirror to study his reflection. There had been a heavy thunderstorm the night before, so all the palace mirrors had been turned to face the wall at the request of the superstitious viscount.

Spires reached up to turn *his* mirror around, and started when the glass fell out of it and shattered into shards on the carpet. He muttered a curse, stepped back from the mess and crouched down to grab a shard large enough to look into. Then, viewing his fractured reflection, he slowly turned his head as he tried to locate the source of the crimson pool he'd been lying in. Odd: he could find nothing that looked or felt even remotely unusual.

Still, there was something wrong, here . . . something missing.

Spires started up another search of the room, but this time he spared no quarter: desk drawers went flying, pictures were taken down and carpet edges were wrenched from the boards beneath them. Nothing.

Except . . .

He hurried over to the fireplace and, crouching down, snaked an arm around the stone. Feeling his way nimbly with thumb and forefinger, he dislodged the palace deeds that had been secreted inside the fireplace since Viscount Curfew's ascendancy. Finding the scrolls intact, he carefully replaced them.

No theft, then. So what on Illmoor was wrong?

Spires desperately tried to think, but it was only when he closed his eyes that the missing element presented itself.

Silence. There was absolutely no noise from the corridor.

Gasping with the realisation, Spires darted forward and flung the portal wide. His personal sentry guard, a stout fellow called Morkus, was struggling to his feet, using a chair to pull himself upright.

'Wh-what's wrong, Mr Secretary, sir? What is it?'

Spires looked down at the carpet, which was stained where the man had been lying.

'I didn't fall asleep, sir! Honest! I just—'

'Woke up? Yes, so did I. Can you remember anything?'

The guard thought for a moment, then shook his head.

'I must've hit me noggin, sir. Sorry about the blood, there . . . I'll get it cleaned up.'

Spires nodded.

'Yes, you will . . . on your way out.'

'Sir?'

'You're fired.'

The guard looked suddenly bewildered.

'Wh-what?'

'You heard me.'

'Wh-what do you mean, sir?'

'I mean exactly what I say, Morkus. YOU. ARE. FIRED.'

Morkus raised a shaking hand to his chin.

'B-but, sir, you said you'd only just woken up yourself!' he managed. 'S-so we were both sort of out, weren't we, sir?'

'That's true,' Spires conceded. 'But, then again, I'm not supposed to be protecting the royal secretary, am I?'

Morkus's lower lip began to tremble, and Spires noticed for the first time how young the man was.

'P-please, sir! I really, really need this job!'

The secretary grimaced.

'Well, you should've thought of that before you allowed yourself to be . . . overcome.'

'I don't know what to say, sir! I've never done anything like this before. I don't even *remember* being tired, sir. I don't remember . . . *anything*!'

Spires gave a cruel smile.

'Well, I'll tell you what, Mighty Morkus, we'll just take a stroll around the palace and if we find the entire guard complement lying unconscious at their posts, you can keep your job. How does that sound?'

'S-sir?'

'You heard me. Pick up your sword and FOLLOW.'

Spires turned and marched determinedly away.

'Come on, man! Don't dawdle.'

Morkus fumbled for his blade and trailed after the secretary, who had picked up his pace and was striding down the corridor like an enraged flamingo.

'I mean, it's not a particularly difficult job!' he muttered, gesturing for the guard to keep up. He rounded a bend in the passage and started down the palace stairs. 'I mean, all you're expected to do is stand outside my room, that's one lone door and a single solitary occupant that you have to attend. Now, as tasks go, it's not what you'd call Herculean, is it?'

'N-no, sir. But—'

'Give me no buts, Morkus. The chips are down. You failed.'

'Y-yes, sir. I know, sir. But still—'

'That's the problem with people like you, Morkus: you want something for nothing. You expect to be paid for a job at which you prove yourself entirely incomp—'

Spires stopped at the foot of the stairs, his feet rooting so quickly that Morkus almost bowled into him.

Not only was the palace's giant portcullis raised, but the gate guards were all slumped in a crumpled heap beneath it, half asleep and – by the look of things – bleeding from the ears. Several were stirring and a few were beginning to get to their feet, but it seemed that *all* of them had been affected.

Spires staggered back, raising a hand to cover his mouth.

'Wh-what – how?'

He spun on his heels, and snatched the shocked guard by his throat.

'The alarm . . . NOW!'

Determined to save his job, Morkus moved faster than he'd ever moved in his life, pelting across the hall and landing on the pull-rope in a frenzied leap. Bells erupted from every direction, piercing the silence and echoing through the shadowy halls of the palace.

As the stout guard continued to throw his weight into the task, Spires retreated back up the stairs and hurried around the palace's plush landing towards the viscount's bedroom. When he arrived at the immense double doors, he soon wished he hadn't. Both of Curfew's elite room guards were semi-conscious.

Spires didn't bother to check the men for wounds, he simply snatched a sword from the nearest guard, threw open the doors and rushed inside . . .

Part Two

The Investigation

One

Enoch Dwellings, the youngest and in his own mind the Most Gifted Detective in the History of Illmoor, clicked across the floor of his study and slumped down on a rickety stool beside the fireplace.

'So this is what I'm reduced to,' he snapped, folding the letter he'd been reading and tossing it into the crackling flames. When the letter had diminished to nothing, he turned to his colleague and mimicked: ' "Dear Mr Dwellings, I'm terribly sorry to bother you but I haven't seen my dog for two days." '

'Ha ha! Fantastic, Enoch! You've got to take *that* one on . . .'

Doctor Edward Wheredad stepped from the shadows

of the room and presented his friend and colleague with a welcome cup of coffee. He was tall and stout with thick lips and a moustache that didn't seem to know when it was beaten. He also had a put-upon look, which was mainly due to the fact that his parents had given him such a dreadful name: most of the people he was introduced to thought he was a doctor.

'I'm absolutely *serious*,' said Dwellings, accepting the coffee with an appreciative nod. 'I tell you; this is no laughing matter! Since that half-breed vampire opened his doors, we've been steadily going out of business. If this drought continues, I'll have to consider downsizing.'

Wheredad, who'd been in the process of returning to his own steaming mug, stopped dead.

'Downsizing?' he echoed. 'But there's only the two of us here!'

Dwellings raised an eyebrow.

'Precisely, my friend. And considering the fact that I'm hardly likely to sack myself, I think we both recognise the implication . . .'

Wheredad's face fell, and he gave a resigned nod.

'Do you want me to leave now?' he hazarded.

Dwellings boggled at him.

'You? Leave? Now? Oh goodness no, I wouldn't hear of it.'

The assistant heaved an audible sigh of relief.

'Thank the gods for that, Enoch. For a moment there I thought . . .'

'Lunchtime would be fine.'

'Mmm? What?'

'I'm not discussing it, Wheredad. I absolutely insist that you stay here for the morning. What sort of heartless employer do you take me for, slinging a man out on to the street at ungodly hours in the pouring rain?'

'B-but we've worked together for ten years!'

'I know, my friend . . . and I have to be honest: I'm absolutely sick to the back teeth of you.'

'I— what? What do you mean?'

Dwellings sighed, then abruptly tossed the remains of his coffee into the fire and leaped to his feet.

'I hate your face. I mean, I try to be polite about it most of the time but, honestly man, have you ever wondered why women never go out with you?'

'I—'

'It's because they can't *SEE* you under there. You're like a great big hairy pie.'

'How dare—'

'And please, please don't keep referring to your "young lady" from Recklans' Inn.'

'Now, look here: Marsha and I—'

'There is no Marsha, Wheredad! I know because I visited the owners when she failed to turn up to dinner for the forty-seventh time! D'you know what they told me? They told me that Marsha is the name they give to the specials menu they parade around the city. Do you understand what I'm saying? You're actually *inventing* a relationship with a *sandwich board* ... exactly how low can you sink?'

'You've never had a girlfriend either!'

Dwellings' gaunt features winced at the observation.

'No, no I haven't ... and I can't help but wonder why!'

'It's – er – it's because you're so busy, Enoch,' Wheredad managed, wondering if he'd gone too far.

'Busy?' Dwellings exclaimed. 'Ha! Not these days, old friend, and certainly not since Obegarde opened his accursed detective agency NEXT BLOODY DOOR!'

Without warning, he rushed over to the far wall and began hammering insanely at the plaster.

THUD.

'*Cut-down prices*, my foot! *Weekly specials*! *Your cheating husband caught or your money back*! *Two investigations for the price of one*! You're a damn, stinking disgrace to the trade, you bloodsucking fiend, you!'

THUD. THUD.

'Haven't got the guts to face me one on one, have you? I've solved more cases than you've had necks, you sissy fingered son of a...'

THUD. THUD. THUD.

Wheredad, now red with embarrassment, waited for his employer's temper to abate. When, after several minutes, Dwellings still showed no signs of fatigue, he went to fetch his coat . . . and walked right into a near-frantic royal page.

'E-e-enoch Dwellings?'

The boy was so out of breath, he was almost crying. He'd evidently stripped off most of his uniform – highly irregular for a palace official – and was literally dripping with sweat. This wasn't entirely surprising: Dwellings' house was a good distance from the palace.

'P-please, sir. You've got to come to the palace at once . . .'

Wheredad spun around, but the wall thumping had ceased, and Enoch Dwellings was already standing to attention, his arms folded and his face bearing an almost sympathetic grin.

'What's the problem, young man?'

The page leaned against the door-frame, and coughed a few times.

'It – it's the viscount, sir.'

Dwellings raised an eyebrow.

'Lord Curfew?'

'Y-yes, sir. We think he's been kidnapped.'

'Oh, don't be ridiculous,' Wheredad chimed, eyeing the boy dubiously. 'The palace has more guards than—'

'Knocked out, sir, and not just the guards – all of us! Cooks, maids, lookouts, even the royal secretary.'

Dwellings pursed his lips, then disappeared for a moment and returned with a grey coat slung over his arm.

'What time is it?' he said, reaching for his watch before anyone could answer. It was a strange habit, and one that Wheredad found increasingly annoying.

'Nearly seven o'clock,' the assistant confirmed, redundantly.

'Early,' Dwellings muttered. He made to march out of the room, and then stopped to grab the page's arm. 'Am I the – that is, did you speak to anyone else before coming here?'

The page shook his head.

'Oh no, sir.'

'And this is the first place you came to?'

'Yes, sir. Well, I did try to get in next door, but he was closed for lunch.'

Wheredad gasped. 'At seven o'clock in the morning? I know he's a vampire, but that's ridic—'

'Shut up, will you?' Dwellings turned from his assistant and glared at the boy.

'WHY did you go there first?'

'I – I'm sorry, sir,' the page stammered. 'But Mr Spires *knows* Mr Obegarde. Besides, he told me to get the best deal I could find and it says on his door that he's doing a special on kidnappings: two for fifty crowns . . .'

While Dwellings gritted his teeth, Wheredad took hold of the page and shoved him roughly through the door.

'Get moving, boy. You can explain everything on the way to the palace. Now, let's see about getting a coach, shall we?'

Two

Morning found Dullitch a sight to behold. From the gleaming Diamond Clock Tower on Crest Hill to the reaching spires of the palace, from the dirt-encrusted outer wall, bristling with barbs and spikes, to the great dome of the New Druid Temple, the city basked in the new day. Most of its inhabitants, however, were still nestled comfortably under their blankets.

The girl entered the cellar by the only door, closing it behind her to shut out the early morning sunlight. It wasn't that the light bothered him all that much but, still, tradition was tradition.

Striking up a match, she felt her way down the stairs, using what little support the rotting banisters afforded.

Then, stepping carefully through the shadows, she arrived at the coffin, knelt down, and rapped sharply on the lid.

'Mmott?' came a muffled reply.

The girl sighed, and swept a lock of blonde hair from her forehead.

'It's him next door, Mr Obegarde,' she started. 'He's just gone tearing up to the palace in a coach.'

There was a moment of strained silence, then the coffin lid flew open, almost knocking the girl unconscious in the process, and a large figure sat bolt upright in the gloom.

'He's up to something,' said the vampire detective, stroking his jagged chin. 'What sort of coach was it?'

The girl shrugged.

'I don't know, Mr Obegarde, I wasn't here, but the woman from the blacksmith's told me that it was a royal page who came for them, and that he knocked at your door first.'

Obegarde glared at her.

'And *you* were out?'

'*Yes*, sir: I don't start until half-seven, remember?'

'Of all the pathetic excuses . . .'

The vampire leaped from his coffin, pushed past the girl and began stomping angrily across the room. 'I tell you, *young lady*, if you've lost me a case, you're out of a job: plain and simple.'

The girl rolled her eyes.

'My name, as I've told you repeatedly, is Lusa, and you can't fire me because you don't pay me anything!'

'I don't?'

'No.'

Obegarde hesitated.

'Then why do you work here?'

'Hmm, that's a good point.' Lusa got to her feet and stood, hands on hips, considering the question. 'Well, I think I come here partly because of the excitement, the mystery, the incredible midnight chases, the romance and the total respect I'm shown by my employer, but mostly because you've kidnapped my damn cat and won't tell me where he is UNLESS I WORK HERE TILL CHRISTMAS!'

Obegarde smiled, his teeth flashing in the gloom.

'Ah,' he said. 'You're *that* Lusa. Get me a coffee, will you?'

'No.'

'Six sugars.'

'I'm not doing it.'

'Fine.' Obegarde offered her another shark-tooth grin. 'I'll tell my people to off Tiddles then, shall I?'

Lusa gasped.

'You wouldn't dare . . .'

'Place your bets!'

'You vicious—'

'Heartripper? Bloodsucker? LOFTWING?' Obegarde

held up his hands. 'Please don't bother: I really have heard them all before. Now, about that coffee . . .'

'No.'

Lusa folded her arms and looked defiant.

'Fine,' said Obegarde, bitterly. 'I'll make it myself, but afterwards I need you to come with me to the palace and sneak inside: we have to find out what's going on with Dwellings and that divvy friend of his. Agreed?'

'Hmm . . . on one condition.'

'Which is?'

'I want to know that Tiddy's safe and well.'

Obegarde gritted his teeth.

'Look,' he growled. 'Unless you start cooperating, you'll get *Tiddy* back one whisker a week, understand me?'

The girl gave a reluctant nod.

'Good. Now fetch that coffee, will you? I'm absolutely parched.'

When Enoch Dwellings arrived at the palace, Secretary Spires was already on the forecourt, wearing a thick coat and a grim smile. He didn't seem to notice that Obegarde wasn't among the emerging company.

'Welcome, gentlemen. Thank you for coming so quickly.'

Dwellings, alighting from the coach he'd hailed at great effort, took a deep breath before he replied.

'Mr Obegarde—'

'Sends his apologies,' Wheredad cut in, shooting his friend a significant look while stamping heavily on the page's foot. 'But he's not very well at the moment. Therefore, he's left this case in the more than capable hands of his – erm – colleague, the remarkable Enoch Dwellings.'

The detective took a theatrical bow and smiled humourlessly.

'I am at your command, secretary. This,' he glanced sideways, 'is my assistant, the admirable Doctor Wheredad. We will assist you in any way we can.'

Spires looked extremely doubtful, but his anxiety eventually won out.

'All right,' he began, his voice still shaky from the effects of his unexplainable unconsciousness. 'But you must first understand that anything you see or hear within the palace walls must be kept strictly confidential.'

Dwellings nodded.

'Of course.'

'Yes, absolutely,' added Wheredad, quietly thanking the gods for their swift intervention in his professional life. 'We understand that the viscount is missing?'

Spires sighed.

'It's so much worse than that,' he muttered, starting up the palace steps. 'Follow me, please.'

The bedroom of Viscount Curfew was a seriously grand affair, with golden trim around every chair and silver curtains allowing light to spill gloriously across an elaborate, diamond-encrusted four-poster. The room itself was an elegant reminder that Dullitch had prospered considerably under the reign of Lord Curfew, though the room's finery owed more to the rising taxes than the many trade opportunities its venerable occupant had created.

The many splendid features of the room were nevertheless slightly marred by the blood.

'Great gods, Enoch,' Wheredad gasped, staring around the bedroom with frank astonishment. 'The stuff's everywhere! Can there be any blood left in the man, do you think?'

Dwellings did his best to mask a look of absolute horror, but when his eyes met those of the royal secretary he simply *had* to look away.

'The room is exactly as I found it this morning,' Spires pointed out, his voice trembling.

Dwellings pursed his lips, and looked upon the secretary as kindly as he could.

'The viscount is your friend?' he asked.

'Yes.' Spires put a hand to his throat, as if he was finding it difficult to swallow. 'I was appointed when Lord Curfew ascended the throne following the Rat Catastrophe. We've – um – we've worked together for a very long time.' He glanced up at the blood on the walls, and his face fell. 'I don't know who or *what* could have done this . . .'

42

Dwellings nodded.

'Leave that to us, Mr Spires,' he said. 'Now, what time did this morning's events begin to unfold?'

Spires gave a shrug.

'I arrived in my office at six o'clock yesterday evening.'

There was a brief pause in which Dwellings looked momentarily bewildered.

'So when did all this take place?' he hazarded. 'Last night or this morning?'

'It's hard to tell,' Spires admitted. 'The last thing I remember is . . . erm . . . I think—'

'So you started your duties last night,' Dwellings interrupted, trying to get things straight in his own head. 'The guards were all awake then?'

'Yes; that is, the ones I saw en route to my office. I live in the palace, you see, so I've no cause to go past the portcullis, last thing.'

'You don't have supper in the kitchens?'

'No. It's usually brought to me by a maid at nine o'clock sharp.'

'And it wasn't last night?'

Spires shrugged.

'I can't remember; I must've been unconscious by then. *She* says she didn't bring me supper; apparently she was out, too.'

'Along with the entire guard force.'

Spires nodded.

'Yes, so it would seem.'

'You don't remember seeing anybody in the room prior to your blackout?' Wheredad cut in, having concluded his scrutiny of the bedchamber's blood-covered walls.

'Not a soul. I distinctly remember looking up at the clock at about a quarter to nine: I was very hungry last night.'

Dwellings pursed his lips, turned to Wheredad.

'We need to speak to the supper maid—'

'I've done that at length,' Spires interrupted. 'As I said before, she *says* that she awoke with the rest of the kitchen staff at six-thirty, soon after I did.'

'Reliable girl, is she?'

'Extremely. She's my niece.'

'Ah.' Dwellings took a deep breath, then strode twice around the room before coming to a reluctant halt beside the bed. 'I assume there's a ransom note . . . ?'

Spires shook his head.

'I wouldn't have worried so much if there was,' he muttered. 'In fact, it's the sheer lack of any kind of motive which has got me shaking, Mr Dwellings. I can't think of any reason why somebody would do this; unless, of course, the perpetrator is working for a rival kingdom.'

'Yes,' Dwellings conceded. 'Or someone who wishes us all to think that it is the work of a rival kingdom. Our relations with Phlegm? Legrash? Spittle?'

'All good: actually, it would be fair to say that they've

never been better. Prince Blood and Earl Visceral are both trading; even King Teethgrit is in productive talks with our merchant lords.'

'I see.'

'So what we're probably dealing with,' Wheredad hazarded, 'is your common or garden variety continental conspirator? The "let's all have a war" sort?'

Spires stared straight at him.

'I'm sure I don't know, Doctor. How many "common or garden variety conspirators" are capable of taking out an entire guard unit and countless palace attendants while at the same time kidnapping a viscount (who, I might add, is probably the best swordsman in the entire city) and escaping completely undetected? Only, I've made a list of the "usual suspects" and, so far, I've come up on the wrong side of naught.'

Wheredad smiled politely and began to back away.

'Do forgive my friend, Mr Spires,' Dwellings said, with a wry smile. 'His brain, it seems, has been temporarily detached from his vocal chords.'

Wheredad huffed and puffed under his breath.

'Still,' Dwellings continued, patting the secretary compassionately on the shoulder. 'You will forgive me if I ask a few seemingly pointless questions of my own?'

Spires nodded.

'If it helps.'

'Good. I notice that there's a large mirror in here. Do you have a mirror in your office?'

'What? Oh, yes. Yes, I do.'

'Was it turned to face the wall when you came in this morning, like this one?'

'Yes, yes. They *all* were; it was because of the storm last night: Lord Curfew has a thing about lightning and mirrors. The funny thing is: most of the mirrors and a lot of the ground- and first-floor windows are broken.'

'Hmm ... interesting. Have you checked to see if there's anything missing from the room?'

Spires nodded.

'Of course. Theft was the first thing I thought of when I came round. There wasn't a thing out of place in my office and there's nothing missing here, apart from the obvious.'

There was a sudden crash from the corner of the room. Wheredad, who had returned to the wall in order to examine the mirror more carefully, was now standing amid its shattered remains.

Dwellings rolled his eyes.

'Oh, terrific, Doc. Absolutely splendid work.'

Wheredad hung his head.

'Terribly sorry, Enoch. I just wanted to see if it was cracked or completely shattered ...'

'... and now we'll never know, will we?' finished Spires, who'd taken an immediate dislike to the man.

'Again, please accept my apologies, Mr Spires. My assistant is not long for this world. At least, he won't be if he continues TO PLAGUE MY VERY EXISTENCE!'

'I-I'll wait outside, Enoch,' said Wheredad, avoiding eye contact with either of the two men as he mooched from the room.

Dwellings took one last cursory glance around the chamber.

'You'll have no objections to us questioning the staff?' he enquired.

Spires shook his head.

'None at all.'

'Then I'd very much like to set up a temporary interrogation room, if it's not too much trouble.'

'You can use the kitchens,' said Spires. 'But do be discreet, I implore you. We don't want the entire city finding out about this before we've had time to prepare an official statement . . .'

'Of course not.' The detective strode out into the corridor. 'Wheredad! Come now; we're going to talk to the guards.'

Three

A terrible clash of swords, steel flying against steel . . . and the blood. Oh, the blood . . .

Eventually, the nightmare subsided . . .

. . . and Viscount Curfew awoke to find himself attached to the wall in what he assumed to be a subterranean cell. He felt weak, as if all his blood had been drained from him.

The nightmare had felt more like a memory; certainly he could remember many things: a pitched sword battle with an assassin who'd entered his bedchambers, the endless clash of swords . . . and the pain.

As Curfew shook himself from his reverie, the cell echoed with the sound of distant laughter.

He peered around. Apart from two great chains securing him to the brickwork, he was bound and gagged and his ankles were locked in a curious wooden device with bells attached to it.

On reflection, it was a great pity that they hadn't bothered to blindfold him. Then he might not have been able to see the gaping pit in the cell floor, or, more importantly, the skeleton chained up next to him; the one wearing Duke Threefold's eagle ring.

Duke Threefold had been ruler of Dullitch long before he'd been born, and even preceded the likes of Vitkins by a good few years. At the end of his reign, he'd disappeared and no one had ever heard from him again.

Curfew trembled at the thought, but quickly reprimanded himself for doing so. He *had* to think straight; otherwise, he was doomed.

But who had brought him here? The intruder he'd fought at the palace?

One point was certain: someone or some*thing* had breached the palace defences and kidnapped him – that sort of situation either took the kind of courage that didn't have a brain or the kind that had more than one.

He flinched in the darkness, and his back began to hurt. Curfew shook himself until the pounding in his head subsided; he *had* to do something . . . and fast. Moving his jaw in a circular motion, he was able to work off the gag.

'Is there anybody out there?' he managed, addressing

the wall where he believed the door to be. He thought that he heard a very distant echo. 'Listen, whoever you are, whatever it is whoever they are're paying you, my people will double it. D'you hear me?'

Silence . . . and the drip, drip, drip of water.

Curfew took a deep breath, and repeated the entire statement. Twice.

His words echoed away.

Drip.

Drip.

Drip.

Curfew licked his dry, cracked lips and sighed: on top of everything else, his head was killing him.

The gatehouse guard frowned, scratched his stubbly chin.

'So when was this appointment arranged?' he asked, doubtfully.

'I beg your pardon?'

'When were you called to the palace?'

'Oh, about five minutes ago. I would have taken my time, but the viscount's secretary said it was an emergency.'

'Secretary Spires?'

'That's him: we're . . . good friends.'

The guard sniffed, belched.

'Who did you say you were again?'

'Obegarde,' said Obegarde, patiently. 'Private Investigator, first class . . . and this is my lovely assistant, Carol.'

'It's Lusa, damn it!'

Obegarde offered her a wry smile by way of an apology, then turned back to the guard.

'So, are you going to let us in or what?'

'I don't know,' the sentry muttered, eyeing both parties dubiously. 'I haven't heard anything about a *second* investigator being called: in fact, I was told on no account to admit *anybody* this morning.'

'Oh, I see.' The vampire shrugged. 'It's just that I'd hate you to get into trouble for not allowing us to enter: I hear the viscount's pretty hot on sacking people at the moment, and it looks like you could really use the money.'

'Yeah, well, I'll risk it.'

'You're a brave man.'

The guard nodded.

'A damn sight braver than you, I'll wager.'

'You reckon?'

'Hell yeah.'

Obegarde pursed his lips.

'Brave enough to let me through?'

The guard shook his head.

'I don't spell brave s-t-u-p-i-d.'

'I know,' Obegarde agreed. '*You* probably spell it c-o-w-a-r-d.'

The guard drew himself up to his full height and stepped in front of the vampire.

'Look, pal, you ain't going in and that's all there is to it, so don't try and bait me with any of that chicken nonsense.'

'OK, fine! I don't want any trouble.'

Obegarde took a step back and put up his hands in a conciliatory gesture.

'Very wise,' said the guard, returning to his post. It was then he noticed that something was wrong.

'Oi,' he snapped at Obegarde. 'Didn't you have a young girl with you a minute ago?'

The vampire nodded.

'Where'd she go?'

'Palace,' said Obegarde. 'Spelled p-a-l-a-c-e. Quick, isn't she?'

Enoch Dwellings pulled an old stool up to the kitchen workbench and rested his chin on his hands.

'So you were the only guard in the entire palace to remain awake throughout the night?' he said, addressing the small and rather dishevelled-looking sentry whose base of operations centred on the High Tower. 'Doesn't that strike you as strange?'

The guard's face flushed red.

'Well, yes, but I've no explanation for it, sir.'

'You *are* human, I take it?'

'Indeed, sir.'

'No elfin blood?'

'No.'

'No dwarf ancestry or greenskin descent?'

'No, sir. My mother's family are cobblers from Spittle, and my father was born a beggar in Legrash.'

'Right. So – tell me about your duties last night.'

The guard pursed his lips.

'Same as usual, sir: keeping watch from the High Tower. I started early last night, 'cause I knew there would be deliveries and stuff. Then the storm started, and I put my earplugs in and—'

'EARPLUGS?' Dwellings seized on the words like an eagle swooping on a field mouse.

'Yes, sir. I'm frightened of thunder, sir: makes me shaky.'

The detective's grin had ignited.

'Doesn't putting earplugs in prevent you from doing your duty?'

The guard shrugged.

'Not really, sir. I can still *see*. Besides, I'm not the only person in the palace who's frightened of thunder: Viscount Curfew don't like it much, either.'

'Does *he* wear earplugs?'

'I wouldn't know, sir, but he was kind enough to give 'em to me a few months back, when I told him how nervous I get.'

Dwellings shared a knowing smile with Wheredad.

'And you alone stayed awake?' he said, turning back to his witness.

The guard gave a nod.

'If you say so, sir,' he managed, his eyes fixed firmly on his shoes. 'I don't s'pose I realised what was going on.'

'And you saw and heard nothing?'

The man shrugged.

'Nothing of any note, sir. There was someone shoutin' abuse at a cat, but you always get that in Dullitch of a night.'

Dwellings tapped his forehead.

'What about deliveries?'

'As I said ... there were a couple earlier in the evening,' the guard continued. 'But neither of 'em were anything to write home about.'

Dwellings nodded, turned to Wheredad.

'Did the gatehouse shift mention any deliveries?' he whispered.

Wheredad consulted his notepad, his thick lips mumbling as his eyes followed the twisty lines of his own scribble.

'Er ... yes, Enoch. One of vegetables, six o'clock sharp, and one of dustsheets at just gone eight.'

Dwellings drew in a breath, then returned his attention to the guard.

'Good man; thank you very much for your time.'

He stood and motioned to the senior guard stationed beside the door.

'Sergeant, do we still have any members of last night's gatehouse crew waiting outside?'

The sergeant nodded, leaned out of the door and yelled at a stout, sombre-faced guard who promptly waddled into the room.

'Do have a seat.'

'Yes, sir,' said the guard, taking his rest.

'Now, er, Private, I'd like you to tell me a little bit about the two deliveries that arrived while you were on guard duty last night.'

The guard scratched his cannonball head.

'What d'you wanna know?' he grunted.

Dwellings chewed his lip, thoughtfully.

'Hmm . . . well, let us begin with the vegetable cart; who was driving it?'

The guard sniffed.

'The veg bloke, sir.'

'The . . . ?'

'Veg bloke. He brings the cart every few days, and tends to make a nuisance of himself afterwards: hangs around the palace for hours, talkin' to folk who're busy workin'. He's a good sort, though; sometimes lets me have the odd lettuce off the back, 'fyou know what I mean.'

'Yes, yes, I think so.' Dwellings nodded. 'Is it always the same "bloke" who brings the cart?'

'Always.'

'Never anyone else . . . ?'

'No.'

'I see . . . And what about the second delivery,

the dustsheets one? What was that all about?'

The guard squinted with the terrible effort that the recollection required.

'They came just before eight o'clock, sir, brought a load o' dustsheets: we checked it over to make sure there was nothing dodgy in it, then admitted 'em.'

'Dustsheets,' Dwellings repeated. 'You mean the sort used for painting?'

'Yeah.'

'And what is it that's being painted?'

'Eh?'

Dwellings rolled his eyes.

'Well,' he continued, 'I assume there's some big painting project underway?'

'I wouldn't know, sir,' the guard admitted. 'But the palace is a big place; there's *always* something being painted round here.'

Dwellings nodded.

'Did you know them?'

'Dunno, sir. That is, I'm not sure what firm they were from.'

'So you didn't recognise *any* of them?'

'You kiddin' me, sir? Dullitch is crawlin' with folk!'

'Granted, but they don't all try to gain entrance to the palace, now DO THEY?'

'Don't s'pose so, no.'

'Right: so what did they look like, these delivery men?'

The guard whistled between his teeth.

'Weeell, the driver was a big fella, must 'ave been well over six foot, lot o' hair; but the other bloke was a shifty-lookin' sort – I didn't like 'im one bit.'

Dwellings glanced at Wheredad, who was scribbling furiously in his pad.

'I think we've got that,' he said, when he was sure the assistant had caught up. 'Do go on.'

The guard gave a disgruntled shrug.

'That's about it,' he said. 'I waved them inside, waited a few minutes for Jiff to lower the gate, and went back to me post. Then I heard this really high-pitched scream, and must've passed out.'

Dwellings clasped his hands behind his head and puffed out a long sigh.

'So these so-called delivery men were definitely *inside* the palace when the scream sounded?'

'Definitely.'

'Thank you very much for your time, Private.'

The guard struggled to his feet and slumped out of the room.

'Interesting, eh?' Wheredad prompted, leaning towards Enoch with a sinister smirk on his face. 'You reckon the delivery men were in on it?'

Dwellings nodded.

'The scream could only be the death cry of a Jenacle banshee,' he whispered. 'Doesn't take much working out, really; at least, not if you know your supernature. Only a banshee death cry would account for the shattered mirrors, the broken windows, the bleeding ears and the induced sleep. Still, don't say anything yet . . . we want to make this case as dramatic as possible before we solve it.'

'Got you,' Wheredad whispered, then said aloud: 'NOT MUCH TO GO ON, BUT AT LEAST IT'S A START . . .'

'Er . . . Mr Dwellings,' said a tall and rather officious-looking guard with four stripes on his arm. 'We found a dead guard on the roof this morning; I don't know if it's related, but—'

'Of course it'll be related, you moron!' Dwellings cried, leaping up from his seat. 'A dead guard? On the roof! Why on Illmoor did no one mention this before?'

The guard shrugged.

'You didn't ask.'

Dwellings closed his eyes and began to count sheep. When the third one had broken its legs trying to get over the spiked fence, he opened them again.

'*Who* was found dead on the roof?' he enquired, politely.

'Tikki LaVale, sir. Guard Marshal of the outer wall.'

'Hmm . . . if he was supposed to be guarding the outer wall, what was he doing on the palace roof?'

'Dunno, sir, but it was a stab wound that did for him.'

Several of the guards looked up in surprise, a gesture that Dwellings picked up on immediately.

'Why the alarm, gentlemen?' he asked, looking from the assembled group to the guard who had originally spoken.

'Well, it's just that Tikki was a really good swordfighter.'

'Yeah,' agreed another. 'I can't think of many better, can you?'

There was a general murmur of agreement.

'Right,' said Dwellings, standing up and pulling on his overcoat. 'Now, is that absolutely *everything* you've told me?'

A series of nods and grunts indicated the positive.

'Good.' He turned to Wheredad. 'Now, let us go back to the office; we've got some— WHAT IN THE NAME OF MERCY IS *SHE* DOING HERE?'

Dwellings suddenly stormed out of the room and hurtled along the corridor, eventually screeching to a halt beside a chattering guard and the innocent but ever-so-pretty girl he'd been talking to.

'You!' Dwellings snapped, thrusting an accusing finger in Lusa's face. 'You're that girl who works for the vampire! Carol, isn't it? What're *you* doing here?'

Lusa tried to smile.

'My name is Lusa,' she said, 'though I'm beginning to realise that it's a *very* difficult name to remember – and I work *with* the vampire, not for him.'

'But what are you doing in the palace?' Dwellings repeated, trying to stay calm. 'Are you working here?

Are you here for *him*? This is *my* case, understand? MINE.'

'OK, OK! I'm just interested, that's all.'

'Well, don't be!' Dwellings motioned to the guard sergeant, who headed straight towards them.

'I'm sorry,' Dwellings said, turning back to the girl. 'But if you're not here on any kind of official business, I'm afraid I'm going to have to ask you to leave.'

Lusa shrugged.

'I don't see why; I just popped in to see my sister.'

Dwellings narrowed his eyes .

'Your sister works here?'

'Yes, and my mother.'

'What's her name?'

'My mother?'

'Your sister.'

'Helen.'

'Helen what?'

'Spinnet.'

'Helen Spinnet—'

'Janeway. '

'What?'

'Janeway,' Lusa repeated. 'It's my sister's third name.'

'Helen Spinnet Janeway—'

'Robinson.'

'Robinson?'

'Yes.'

'Your sister's name is Helen Spinnet Janeway Robinson?'

'That's right.'

'What's your mother called, Mary Margaret Quicksoak Quackbuster?'

Lusa glared at him.

'Don't you make fun of my family!'

'Are you serious? That's her name?'

'You must know it is!'

'What? That was a complete guess!'

'Don't be ridiculous.'

'I swear!'

Lusa grinned.

'Well, that's her name,' she said, trying not to smile. 'She's a chambermaid, and my sister works in the kitchens.'

'What floor?'

'I'm sorry?'

Dwellings smiled evilly.

'What floor does your mother the chambermaid work on?'

'The fifth.'

'There isn't a fifth floor.'

The girl folded her arms.

'Well, technically there *is*, but the viscount's having work done up there, so all the maids have been moved down a level.'

Dwellings glanced at the guard.

'Is that true?' he asked.

'Yeah,' said the man. 'But I've never seen this girl before in my life, and I'm damn sure she doesn't have a sister here: all the maids are ugly.'

Dwellings turned to Lusa and beamed.

'Thank you, guardsman,' he said. 'Now do please escort this young lady off the premises: she has a disgustingly underhanded vampire to report to.'

Five

'Well?' said Obegarde, sighting his assistant and her two
burly escorts. He waited until the guards had retreated
back inside the palace, then hurried her beyond the
nearest wall. 'Did you get anything?'

'Not from the hierarchy; I didn't get a chance to
eavesdrop. There's a mass interrogation going on.' Lusa
made a face that Obegarde guessed correctly.

'Dwellings?' he hazarded.

Lusa gave an exasperated nod.

'He's serious about this vendetta thing the two of you
have going. He said it's "his" case and no one else is
getting a look-in.'

'Ha! We'll see about that . . .'

Lusa looked glum.

'He's not too bright, though. He definitely would've fallen for my family-at-the-palace story if some idiot guard boss hadn't tipped him off.'

Obegarde gritted his teeth, and slumped against the wall.

'Did you manage to glean anything?' he asked hopefully.

Lusa smiled.

'I got talking to one of the junior guards,' she said. 'He says there was an incident at the palace last night. There's a rumour going around that the viscount's been kidnapped.'

'Kidnapped?' Obegarde suddenly realised that he was beginning to draw attention from the market traders, so he took Lusa by the arm and led her away from the hustle and bustle.

'Are you sure?' he whispered, trying to sound as casual as possible under the weight of such significant news.

Lusa shook her head.

'No,' she said. 'Like I told you, it's just a rumour running between the guards.'

'It makes sense though, doesn't it?' the vampire continued, struggling to keep the excitement out of his voice. 'I mean, think about it: a page comes knocking on the door of the be— er – second best private investigator in the city; there's a mass interrogation at the palace; and no sign of the viscount! Ha! I'll bet that's it. Good work, Carol; very good work.'

'If you call me that one more time, I'll—'

'. . . never see Tiddles again?' Obegarde grinned. 'You're absolutely right: you *won't*.' He came to a sudden standstill in the middle of North Street and snapped his fingers.

'I need you to go back to the office,' he said, trying to give the girl his most friendly smile. 'When Dwellings and Wheredad return, try to strike up some sort of bargain with them.'

Lusa rolled her eyes.

'Like what?'

'Oh, I don't know! Tell them, er, tell them that Dwellings is a big hero of mine and that I've always wanted to work with him. No, actually, don't tell them that; tell them that I respect him as the stuff of legends and . . . er . . . oh, for goodness' sake MAKE SOMETHING UP!'

'Hang on – what are you going to do?'

'Not much else today, but tomorrow I might look for Jimmy Quickstint.'

Lusa frowned. 'The gravedigger? Why?'

'Because he used to be a thief, and he's probably the only person in Dullitch who can get me into the palace without anyone knowing.'

Obegarde turned and headed back down North Street, his coat billowing out behind him.

Lusa watched him go with a mixture of hate and grudging respect. She didn't quite know what was worse: the fact that he was a despicable, cat-stealing bloodsucker or the fact that he was her despicable, cat-stealing bloodsucker dad. Still, what he didn't know wouldn't hurt him, and she wasn't about to go telling the wretch something like *that*.

At least, not until he'd given the cat back . . .

Lusa had arrived back at the office shortly after four o'clock, but there was still no sign of Dwellings and no one was answering the doorbell, so she'd decided to spend the remaining hour of daylight searching Obegarde's cluttered office for some sign of her cat. She'd gone through this procedure several times before, but so far her searches had turned up little except an old, Tiddles-smelling cushion and two paint-stiffened whiskers next to it. The cushion was a promising clue, but she didn't even want to think about the whiskers . . . He wouldn't actually have dipped the cat in a paint tin, would he?

Time passed, and the shadows lengthened.

Lusa didn't even know *why* she'd wanted to meet her father in the first place. Her mother had had few nice words to say about him, and had told her little apart from the fact that he was a well-built, good-looking vampire in his mid to late hundreds and that he'd moved to Dullitch just before she was born to 'make money for the family while escaping the terror of parenthood'. Ha: what a lie! They'd never seen so much as a brass crown! Still, thankfully, her mother then met and married a Lord and they soon became very wealthy. Lusa had been educated in the top colleges of Spittle and brought up to be a Lady (despite the fact that the finishing school she'd attended had nearly lived up to its name when thirty of her classmates were involved in a fight to the death over the affections of a seriously handsome half-elf gardener).

Still, education was education ... and she'd triumphed. Then, one winter evening like none before or since, she'd asked her mother to tell her about *him*, and she'd been given the bare essentials. She knew immediately that she would have to meet her father, but she didn't want to do it in the normal, everyday 'hi, I'm the daughter you abandoned' kind of way in which people tended to do these things; she wanted to get to know the *man* before she got to know the *father*.

Well, what a flame-grilled disappointment *that* decision had turned out to be. Because now she *did* know the man – and she didn't like him ... not one little bit.

The spiteful, competitive and violent nature she could ignore, but cat-napping? That was the lowest of the low. After all, what kind of deranged, psychopathic lunatic steals a girl's cat five minutes after meeting her, then *uses* the deed to blackmail her into becoming his secretary for the rest of the year? It absolutely beggared belief, and if Obegarde hadn't been her father, she'd have gone running to the militia without a second thought.

I still will if he's murdered Tiddles, she told herself determinedly, rummaging through boxes, tearing aside curtains and peering around doors all over the building. *I'll drop him right in it and I won't feel the teensiest bit guilty.*

Then, while searching around on the top floor of the building, she stumbled across the secret wall.

Obegarde's library was a complete fabrication. On the face of things, it looked like your typical professor's library, with sturdy, leather-bound volumes lining the walls on all sides, some of them stacked in dusty bookcases while others stared out from elegant glass cabinets ranged one on top of another. And all of them were made of cardboard.

Lusa couldn't believe her eyes.

She checked again, reaching for the nearest book and picking up the whole row with unreserved ease. She chuckled at the absurdity of it, and at the thought of Obegarde showing people around the room, pretending he was extremely well read and remarkably studious.

It was as she stood there, a mock-row of cardboard books in her hand, that she noticed the one book still standing on the shelf. She immediately reached for it, and stood back in total surprise as half the wall opened up before her.

Lusa took a step back, waited until the portal had swung wide, and stepped through . . .

. . . into the bedroom of Enoch Dwellings.

Lusa didn't realise what had happened immediately; at first, she thought she had stumbled upon a small and secret room that Obegarde might have used for sleeping when he didn't fancy the coffin. The room would certainly have suited a vampire: it had no windows and only a single door which managed to shut out even the merest hint of light from what had to be a landing beyond.

Lusa stood in the quiet gloom, pondering the significance of this find: Obegarde had a secret door into Dwellings' home. Did this explain how he'd been able to steal most of the detective's cases? The more she thought about the idea, the more it made sense. The rich and desperate would turn up at the door of Enoch Dwellings, for it was he who had the reputation, and then Obegarde would sneak in during the night, take down all the details and solve the cases before Dwellings had time to get to them! Ha! Doubtless, he probably pretended to be one of Enoch's assistants into the bargain: the wretch!

Lusa smiled at the discovery, and was just about to creep back through the secret door when she spotted her cat – fast asleep – on a cushion in the far corner of the room.

'Can you believe the audacity of that fiend?' Dwellings exclaimed, heading along the palace corridors as if the hounds of hell were baying for him. 'Sending that young spy of his to steal my case out from under me?'

'It's disgusting, Enoch,' Wheredad panted, making every effort to stay level with his employer. 'I don't know why we stand for it.'

Dwellings stopped dead in the corridor.

'What do you mean?' he said, staring at the assistant from the corners of his eyes. 'We're not standing for it! We're not standing for it at all . . .'

'No, Enoch, of course not: I just meant to say that . . . well—'

'You just meant to say that I'm a fool!'

'No, really I—'

'Well, if I'm a fool, Wheredad, then what does that make you? Assistant to a fool? Apprentice to an idiot? Ha! Well just remember that YOU HAVEN'T HAD A GIRLFRIEND EITHER!'

Wheredad rolled his eyes.

'Why does it always come back to girls, Enoch?' he pleaded. 'Is that really all you think about?'

'Of course it isn't!' Dwellings spat. 'It doesn't bother *me* at all. *You're* the one who keeps mentioning it.'

'But I haven't said—'

'There you go again! Girls, girls, girls! I tell you something: you need a damn good doctor yourself!'

'Really, Enoch. There's no need for that—'

Dwellings held up an admonitory hand.

'Look, let's just focus on the case, shall we?'

'Yes. *Please* let's.'

'We'll ignore the fact that you're obviously head over heels for that girl of Obegarde's.'

'Me?' Wheredad's sudden look of incredulity caught his employer totally unawares. 'I didn't even *see* that girl; *you* were the one talking to her!'

'That's right, Wheredad, pass the blame around. It doesn't change the fact that you're in denial.'

The assistant counted to ten under his breath and checked his pulse. Then he said: 'Look, Enoch. I know I've never had a girlfriend before, but I really, truthfully don't want one at the moment ... and that's the difference between us: I think you *do*.'

Dwellings pursed his lips, sucked in a breath and sighed.

'You're absolutely right, Wheredad,' he said, reluctantly. 'We really should focus all of our attention on the case.'

The assistant let out an exasperated breath, and his shoulders slumped.

'Yes, Enoch,' he said, weakly. 'Let's.'

They'd arrived in the palace courtyard, where several coaches were being painted for the viscount's next public address.

'It's only two weeks away, isn't it?' Dwellings asked one of the decorators.

The man took a pencil-thin paintbrush from behind his ear and squinted back at Dwellings.

'Eh?'

'The duke's next address: it's only two weeks away?'

'Yeah, but don't worry yourself – we'll 'ave all these shipshape by then.'

'Good,' Dwellings said, flashing the man a smile he reserved for people he'd taken an immediate dislike to, 'but it's really not the coaches I'm worried about.'

'Say again?'

'I said "keep up the good work"!'

'Yeah, right.'

The man returned to his patient destruction of the coach and Dwellings idled back to Wheredad.

'So what do we do now, Enoch?' said the assistant, stowing his notepad away in the pocket of his jerkin.

'Hmm . . . an interesting question. I think we should probably look into recent city kidnappings; and I'm almost certain that we should investigate Jenacle banshees, find out where they come from and how rare they are. D'you think you can handle that?'

'Of course, Enoch. I'll get to the library at once!'

'Good, good. I'm going back to talk to Mr Spires about getting some help from the council.'

The royal secretary leaned back in his old oak chair and carefully rubbed his tired eyes with a fingertip.

'I understand your concern, milady, I *really* do,' he said. 'But you must realise that we are doing absolutely *everything* we can to find Rav— his excellency. Apart from all that, you really should be resting: you went through this terrible ordeal the same as everybody else! How is your hearing?'

Contessa Curfew, a tall lady with generous weight behind her and hips that could have supported a platoon of children, blew her nose loudly on the handkerchief she'd been waving in Spires' face.

'I don't think you are up to the task, Spires,' she said accusingly, ignoring the secretary's question. 'If you *were*, we would have heard something by now.'

'Please be patient, milady. Rest assured that Mr Dwellings is on the case and we won't have long to wait before this matter is completely resolved.'

Lady Curfew took another half-hearted blow on her handkerchief.

'Mr who?' she said.

'Mr Dwellings,' said Spires, flinching slightly. 'Enoch Dwellings? The legendary detective?'

'I've never heard of him.'

'No, well, he's very . . . discreet.'

Spires shuffled some papers and made to stand up, his own ever-so-subtle hint that he wanted out of the conversation.

'I'll let you know as soon as I hear anything, milady. You have my word.'

'Very good, Spires.' She turned to leave, then hesitated in the doorway. 'Because, if you don't find my husband and bring those responsible to justice, *I'll* have your *head*.' She gave a final, tearful sigh and departed, leaving the royal secretary muttering bitterly under his breath.

Unfortunately, Spires didn't get much respite: the contessa had only been gone two minutes when Enoch Dwellings made an unscheduled appearance at the office door.

'Excuse me, Mr Spires . . .'

'Yes?'

'I have a favour to ask of you.'

'Is it going to bring back the viscount?'

'It may help.'

The secretary let out a sigh.

'Go on, then.'

'I'm going to need some cooperation from the city council,' Dwellings said, taking a seat at the secretary's desk without being asked. 'I need access to criminal records, daily guard reports and non-Yowler related acts of theft, murder and vandalism.'

'Fine, I'll speak to the chairman immediately.'

'Thank you; still old Sands, is it?'

'Mmm?'

'Quaris Sands? Is he still the council's chairman? I'm afraid I don't tend to keep up with such things.'

'Obviously not: Quaris retired some years ago – I believe he now lives in Legrash. The head of the council is a troglodyte named Burnie. He's not from the same stock as Tambor Forestall or Quaris Sands, but an amiable little fellow nonetheless. When were you thinking of popping in?'

'Tomorrow morning: I have some other inquiries to follow up before then.'

'Very well,' Spires mumbled. 'But do work quickly, I implore you: the contessa is baying for my blood and if Lord Curfew isn't found soon, I fear I'll be first for the chopping block.'

Lusa crept over to the huddled yet recognisably cute form of Tiddles, and stroked him gently behind the ears. Then, whispering to him in the way that all cat owners tend to do when disturbing something that could feasibly remove their face with its claws, she carefully prodded him awake.

'Tiddles?'

An eyelid flicked open, and the cat began to purr.

'Oh it is you! Did he hurt you, baby? I'll kill him if he hurt you . . .'

She had to admit, the cat didn't look that put-out: his fur had been brushed, the basket he'd been sleeping in looked clean and snug, and there were several squeaky toys around the room.

She was about to scoop the cat into her arms when a thought occurred, and instead she replaced it in the squashy confines of its bed. Then, carefully crossing the room on tiptoes, she opened the bedroom door and inched out on to the landing.

The house was quiet, but she listened for several seconds, just to make sure. All she could hear was the rattle of coaches outside and the rhythmic sound of her own breath.

Steeling herself to the task, Lusa dropped down on to her hands and knees and began to examine the ancient floorboards. It didn't take her long to find what she was looking for: a slight yet unmistakable boot-print in the dust. Lusa nodded . . . and a grim but nevertheless determined smile settled on her face.

Seven

Viscount Curfew wasn't accustomed to fear. He was a shrewd swordfighter and a brilliant marksman, and people who dared to engage him in fisticuffs inevitably crawled away on all fours, searching for their teeth. He was also the eldest son of one of the most powerful families in Dullitch, and he had the sort of relaxed attitude towards personal safety that only money can bring about.

However, right now, Viscount Curfew was scared: not by the rhythmic chants resounding around the dungeon, nor by the lion-like roar from the corridor beyond the cell, nor even by the fat snake that had begun to slither underneath the cell door. No, Lord Curfew's particular focus of fear had been drawn to the deep, cavernous hole in the floor of the cell, and to the terrible creature that was emerging from within . . .

As he fought desperately to try to free himself from his bonds, he averted his eyes from the writhing, shapeless mass that was filling the room, feeling its way blindly towards him on bloated tentacles, each with their own slavering tongues and thin, needle-sharp teeth. It spread out further, seeking, searching, until . . .

. . . Viscount Curfew woke up, screaming.

The cell was just as it had been on first sight: there was no hole in the floor, no snake and, more importantly, no monster.

There was only the silence, and the drip, drip, drip.

Eight

It was a new morning in Dullitch, and the city was alive with bustle. Birds twittered among the trees, had stones thrown at them and fell out. Children dashed up and down the cobbles, tripped, hit the cobbles and ran home screaming. Normality reigned.

The coach conveying Enoch Dwellings and his bulky colleague came to a screeching halt outside City Hall, and the two passengers clambered out. Neither man looked particularly happy to be awake, though Wheredad *had* discovered something interesting at the library: Jenacle banshees, it appeared, were currently bred in Crust.

Dwellings paid the coachman and the two men started towards the hall's grand entrance.

Burnie, the troglodyte chairman of the Dullitch Council, was waiting for them at the top of the steps.

'I've spoken to Secretary Spires,' he said, leading them through the large double doors and into a small office on the left. 'Anything you need, just name it.'

Dwellings nodded.

'Thank you. I'd like to see a complete record of any kidnappings that have taken place inside the city walls over the last – oh, I don't know – twelve months?'

'None.'

Dwellings flinched slightly at the abrupt response.

'I beg your pardon?'

'None,' Burnie repeated. 'There haven't been any kidnappings in Dullitch since Diek Wustapha ran off with all the kids during the Rat Catastrophe.'

Dwellings scoffed at him.

'Oh, don't be ridiculous. You're not seriously telling me . . .'

'I am.' Burnie nodded, a wry smile on his mucus-dripping face. 'Not one. Good, isn't it?'

'Murders?'

'Hmm . . . well, we've had plenty of Yowler hits this week, but nothing out of the ordinary – unless, of course, you count the men they found on the cart this morning.'

'Dead?' Wheredad muttered, casting his employer a significant look.

'Yes,' Burnie confirmed, rifling through a stack of scrolls. 'It was reported just after eight o'clock: a guard found two bodies in an old cart. I don't think they count as Dullitch murders, though: the cart was found near the North Gate, on its way in by the look of it, and both blokes were dressed in funny outfits.'

'Spittalian?' Dwellings enquired, his interest suddenly aroused.

Burnie shook his glutinous head.

'No, looked more Western than that, like something they'd wear in Irkesome or Crust.'

'The cart,' Wheredad prompted, sticking doggedly to the points on his notepad. 'It wasn't covered in dustsheets, by any chance?'

The troglodyte councillor consulted the scrolls, unfurling one and staring confusedly at another.

'Sorry,' he said eventually, shaking his head. 'Says here it was a vegetable cart.'

Dwellings caught Wheredad's glance and immediately seized upon it.

'You say the cart was found near the North Gate?' he asked, reaching across to take the scroll from Burnie's gloopy fingers.

''Sright,' said the troglodyte, grimly. 'We're still looking for the chap who owned it.'

'Excellent,' said Dwellings. 'I take it you still have the cart impounded? We need to see it immediately.'

The troglodyte heaved a sigh.

'Fine,' he said. 'But them boys're not a pretty sight, I'm telling you.'

'Where is it?'

'The militia's holding pound,' Burnie muttered. 'I've got some things to do right now, but I can meet you there in about twenty minutes?'

'Jimmy, old friend! How— where are you going? Hey! Come back here!'

Obegarde raced across the cemetery, but Jimmy Quickstint had already shinned up a giant oak tree by the time the vampire arrived, puffing and panting, beside it.

'W-what are you running away from?'

'You!'

'Me? What have I done?'

Jimmy peered down through the branches and thrust an accusing finger at the vampire.

'Last time I got mixed up with you, we ended up in Plunge, fightin' a dark sorceress.'

Obegarde smiled.

'I know – good laugh, wasn't it?'

'Are you serious?'

'No, of course not! Anyway, none of that was my fault! It was old Duke Modeset that dragged us all out there, remember?'

'Yeah, whatever. Just get lost, will you?'

Obegarde shook his head.

'Not until you come down from that tree! Besides, that's no way to talk to a friend!'

'You're not my friend, Obegarde. You're a damn stinkin' nuisance.'

The vampire drew himself up to his full height and bellowed up at the treetop.

'LOOK, AT LEAST HEAR ME OUT! I MIGHT HAVE SOMETHING IMPORTANT TO SAY!'

'Fat chance.'

Obegarde bit his lip and counted to ten. Then he said, very calmly:

'If you don't come down from that tree in the next twenty seconds, I'm going to come up and get you. Understand?'

'Ah, threats now, is it?'

'ONE.'

'I could've guessed as much.'

'TWO.'

'It always comes down to temper with you bloodsuckers.'

'THREE.'

'I'm not coming down.'

'EIGHT.'

'Where'd you learn to count?'

'ELVEN.'

'Elven? That's not a number, that's a race.'

'NINETEEN.'

'OK, now you're just being stupid.'

'TWENTY.'

'I'm just on my way down.'

There was an uncomfortable-looking backward swing followed by a number of yelps and crunches as Jimmy Quickstint fell out of the tree, hitting practically every branch on the way down. Eventually, he hit the ground, dusted himself off and stared up at a very irritated vampire.

'So,' he said, fingering a cut on his bottom lip. 'What are you trying to break into?'

Obegarde took a sudden step back, and studied the gravedigger's expression.

'How did you guess?' he asked, cautiously.

Jimmy shrugged.

'I only have two skills, and I take it you don't want someone buried?'

'Well, actually . . .'

'No chance.'

'I was going to say that you were right first time: I *do* need to get inside a certain place . . .'

'It'll cost you.'

Obegarde shrugged.

'Fine. How much?'

Jimmy seemed to pay serious attention for the first time. His hands came out of his pockets and his tired, put-upon expression changed to one of mild interest.

'That all depends on the property,' he muttered. 'Is it uptown or downtown?'

'It's . . . er . . . central.'

'Does it have a back garden?'

'It has . . . land *round* it.'

'Guarded?'

'Heavily.'

'Hmm . . . how many of you going in?'

'Just me.'

'Night or day?'

'Night, preferably.'

'Right.' Jimmy did some quick mental arithmetic, and seemed to reach a conclusion. 'That'll cost you fifty crowns.'

Obegarde's jaw dropped open.

'Er . . . I said I wanted to *break in*, not buy the joint.'

Jimmy sighed.

'Well, that's the best deal you're going to get out of Quickstint Enterprises.'

'Ten crowns.'

'Get out o' town! I wouldn't break into a dogs' home for that!'

Obegarde thought for a moment.

'Twenty crowns and you can take whatever you find there,' he said, conclusively.

'Done.'

'Shake on it?'

The two men clasped hands to seal the deal, with Obegarde pulling back when he noticed that Jimmy had spat on his first.

'So,' the gravedigger muttered, his trademark grin returning. 'Where is it we're going, exactly?'

'The palace.'

'Say that again?'

'The palace.'

'As in THE PALACE? Viscount Curfew's palace?'

'Uhuh.'

'It's back to fifty crowns, then,' Jimmy said, through gritted teeth. '*They* haven't got anything worth stealing.'

Obegarde rolled his eyes.

'Look, are you in or not?' he demanded, thrusting a finger in the gravedigger's face.

'I'm in.'

'Great. Where shall I meet you?'

Jimmy sighed.

'You know the manhole cover in Royal Road?'

'Yes.'

'Meet me there, stroke o' midnight.'

The gravedigger turned and strode off towards the cathedral, whistling a merry tune.

'Just listen to me, Wheredad. Let's say for now that the kidnappers are from Crust. They take Curfew last night, drive him out of the city via the North Gate, where the guards are probably playing cards, and get him back to their hideout. With me?'

'Yes . . .'

'OK, then *this* morning at eight o'clock the guards find two *Crust* bodies on the same vegetable cart that was in the palace last night. Don't you see what this means?'

'Um . . .'

'It means, numb-brain, that they came back! One or all of the cronies who kidnapped Curfew must have returned to Dullitch this morning! They're here now!'

'B-but why: when they've already got the viscount?'

'*That*, my friend, is what we need to find out.'

Dwellings and Wheredad marched through the crowded streets en route to the militia's holding pound. In the Market Place, they sidled carefully past two quarrelling ogres while at the same time narrowly avoiding a dwarfish slambol team recruitment officer. Sensing that it was likely to be one of *those* afternoons, they quickly headed down Quack Avenue for some peace and quiet.

'So what do you think about the officer they found on the roof, Enoch?' said Wheredad, swinging his thick arms as he walked.

Dwellings shrugged.

'The guards seemed to think a lot of him; so I suspect that the assailant who cut him down was highly adept at swordplay. It's strange, though; we had our suspicions pinned on the cart team, and now there's yet another player in the mix.'

'You mean . . . ?'

'Precisely, Wheredad: I think the *person* on the roof was involved with the group on the cart. We just have to work out how . . . and why.'

Nine

'Well, look here, Tiddles, if it isn't that nice Mr Obegarde!'

The vampire, who'd only just walked through the front door, froze. His head dipped ever so slightly, as if he was expecting a barrage of flying crockery.

Lusa was sitting, cross-legged, at the foot of the stairs, grinning from ear to ear. She was holding Tiddles on her lap.

'Ah, I see you found him, then,' Obegarde muttered, mooching over to his desk. 'How did you manage that?'

Lusa shrugged.

'I investigated,' she said. 'And in case you don't know, "investigate" is when people find things out for themselves, not when they leech and spy on other, better investigators, in order to steal cases from them.'

Obegarde's half-grimace melted away.

'My,' he said. 'But you really have been snooping around, haven't you?'

'Yes. Funny that: I was looking for my cat.' She jumped up from the step and began to walk determinedly towards him. Just think, if I hadn't had to go searching for the pet that *you* stole from me, I'd never have discovered your little doorway into the Dwellings house, now would I?'

'Now look,' said Obegarde, nervously. 'You're not going to tell him, are you?'

Lusa put a finger to her lips and frowned, as if she was mulling over a very difficult problem.

'Tell him what exactly? That a devious, despicable, backstabbing, case-stealing bloodsucker of a vampire has been sneaking into his house each night through a concealed door in his bedroom? Um . . . yes, I actually think I might.'

'Don't you dare!'

'Shut up.'

'If you do—'

'You'll what? You're a loftwing, remember? You've only got the one tooth.'

'Now listen to me. I'm not just going to let you walk in there and—'

'I'm your daughter.'

'That's all very well, but as I said . . . as I said then . . . as I . . . YOU'RE MY WHAT?'

'Daughter.'

Obegarde's jaw practically broke his knees.

'What d'you mean? How on Illmoor can you be my daughter?'

'Um . . . the usual way, probably.'

'B-but . . . but . . .'

Lusa rolled her eyes and allowed some time for her statement to sink in.

Obegarde swallowed a few times. He tried to speak, but his lips were suddenly dry. He hunted around in his desk for the vinegar he always kept handy. Then, after finding the bottle and taking several gulps of the vile liquid, he looked up at the girl beside the stairs.

'You're . . . Audrey's daughter?'

Lusa shook her head, causing Obegarde a moment of anxiety.

'Sarah's daughter?'

'No!'

'You're not Flapjack's daughter, are you?'

'Flapjack?' Lusa gasped. 'You had a . . . relationship . . . with someone called Flapjack?'

'Yes, but don't get melodramatic about it – I was a bat, then.'

'Oh . . . right.'

Obegarde's face had flushed red with embarrassment.

'I have to confess that I don't have the slightest inkling of an idea whose daughter you might be.'

Lusa stopped in the centre of the room, and folded her arms.

'I'm yours,' she said, dispassionately. 'Trust me.'

The vampire hung his head.

'I'm sorry,' he said. 'You ... er ... must be very disappointed.'

Lusa thought about this for a time.

'Not really,' she said, putting her head on one side. 'My mother told me exactly what to expect.'

'Well, whatever she told you . . . it's bound to be true. I'm not a good person. I did sort of help save the country once, but I don't suppose that really evens the score on a one-to-one basis . . .'

'No.'

'Right. So . . . what have you really been doing here, all this time? Reporting back to your mother – whoever she is – about what a terrible cretin I am?'

'No; of course not!'

'Do you need money?'

'No: I need your time.'

Obegarde sighed.

'I don't have any,' he said, weakly. 'Besides, the more we get to know each other, the more you'll hate me!'

'Not necessarily . . .'

'You hate me now, don't you?'

'At the *moment* I do.'

'Exactly, and we've only been working together for three weeks!'

'But I only *hate* you because you stole my cat!'

'So why did you bring it in here in the first place?'

'Because I was new in the city; I didn't know anybody well enough to leave him with!'

'Oh get over it. Anyway, I didn't *steal* the cat!'

'What happened, then?'

Obegarde stomped over to his coffin and slumped down on top of it.

'Well, that day you came in . . .'

'Yes, I remember it clearly. You asked me if I'd work for bread and water.'

'Right, well, when I got up to go to the toilet, your cat followed me.'

'And?'

'And I sort of accidentally led him to the top floor and shoved him through the secret wall.'

'You are a total—'

'Hey, I needed you to work for me!'

'So? You didn't have to kidnap my cat!'

Obegarde gave a half-hearted shrug.

'I thought it was the right thing to do.'

'Ha! What kind of twisted logic is that?'

'The normal kind! Besides, I knew damn well that Dwellings and Whydude would take good care of him.'

'That's beside the point: you still did it, and my first impression of my father was that he was a kidnapper.

Can you imagine how impressed I was when you told me I *had* to work here or you'd harm the cat?'

'I said I'm sorry – what more do you want?'

'I'll tell you what I want, I want YOU to go next door and tell Mr Dwellings exactly what you've been up to for the last . . . for the last however many months you've been doing it!'

'Are you insane? I'll be ruined!'

'Ha! At least you'd have a clear conscience.'

'I've got a clear conscience now!'

Lusa swept back a lock of blonde hair, gritted her teeth.

'If you don't go round there this *instant*, I'm going to tell them everything myself!'

Obegarde let out an exasperated breath.

'All right,' he said, bleakly. 'I'll go. Satisfied?'

'Maybe.'

'Thank the gods for that. Personally, I can't believe I'm being pressured into this. Whose daughter did you say you were?'

Enoch Dwellings stood back as the city militia's personal guard escort wheeled out the vegetable cart and gently lowered its wobbly front end on to the cobbles. The two men were still inside the cart, bound together by a thick rope.

'Crossbow wound?' Wheredad hazarded.

'You think?' said Dwellings, sarcastically. 'I was going for poison, myself.'

Wheredad shook his head.

'No, Enoch, I don't think they'd have shot a bolt through each if they were going to poison them. It wouldn't make any sense . . .'

Dwellings ignored the statement, and instead reached into the cart to examine the men's clothing.

'This is all Crust issue,' he said in conclusion, a few minutes later. 'The boots, the jerkin, all of it.'

'We thought as much,' said Burnie, who'd arrived just in time to accompany the two investigators to the militia's storage yard. 'Strange, though: it's quite a distinctive cart. I had a really good pair of guards on the North Gate that night, and they both swear blind that they saw this cart come and go last night, driven by somebody else entirely.'

'I'll wager it was the one that visited the palace,' Dwellings muttered conspiratorially to Wheredad.

'You reckon so, Enoch?'

'Well, it would be a funny coincidence, wouldn't it?'

Wheredad brought out his notepad and quickly read through his scrawl.

'So we think that the veg bloke drove this cart into town at about—'

'Half-past five,' Burnie interrupted, sharp as a button. 'That's when the guards saw the cart through the gate.'

'Right,' said Wheredad, a little resentfully. 'Then he stopped at the palace at just gone six o'clock, leaving again at . . . ?'

'We didn't ask when he left the palace,' said Dwellings, suddenly annoyed at his own forgetfulness.

'Obviously, I can't help you there,' said Burnie. 'But I *can* tell you that the *cart* went back out of the North Gate just after ten o'clock. The guards were awake, for once. They didn't stop it, mind; probably used to seeing it come and go.'

Dwellings nodded.

'Your help has been invaluable, Mr Chairman,' he said. 'Now, I don't suppose your men have any record of a cart full of dustsheets leaving or entering the city that evening?'

Burnie consulted the scroll he'd brought with him, and shook his head.

'Some hope,' he said, casting a disgruntled glance at the nearest guard-post. 'Some of 'em don't stop playing cards long enough to tie their shoes.'

Dwellings nodded, and turned back to his colleague.

'Wheredad, make a note that the second cart probably came from *outside* the city.' He nodded appreciatively at Burnie and his assistants. 'My thanks go out to you, gentlemen; do come back to me if you think of anything else.'

He bowed slightly and departed, Wheredad trailing in his wake.

Ten

Obegarde swallowed a few times, and straightened himself up. Then he checked out of the corner of his eye to make sure that the wretched girl was still watching him from the bay window and – realising she was – took a reluctant step forward and rapped loudly on the door of Enoch Dwellings.

A few tense seconds passed, in which he actually stepped back from the threshold to prepare himself, but there came no answer from within.

Obegarde made a beseeching grin at his eagle-eyed daughter, then gave a shrug and tried again.

Nothing.

'He's not in,' he called up at the neighbouring window.

Lusa frowned, mouthed something.

'I said: HE'S NOT IN.'

The right-side window was suddenly hoisted open. 'What?'

Obegarde rolled his eyes.

'He's not in.'

'He's out?'

'Yes! Look, I know it's very difficult to understand, but if you're not in, you're out; and if you're not out, you're in. That's the way it works. OK? Now I really have to go: I've promised to meet someone later, and I need to get some sleep . . .'

Lusa took a deep breath, rolled her eyes.

'Well, I suppose you *could* try him later on,' she said.

'You betcha,' said Obegarde, a merry smile on his pale lips. 'I'll be back round here the first chance I get; you can bet your wages on it.'

'You don't pay me any wages . . .'

'Exactly.'

Lusa muttered something under her breath, then folded her arms.

'Leave him a note,' she demanded.

'What? You can't be serious: he'll think I'm out of my tree!'

'Just DO IT.'

Obegarde bit his bottom lip, quickly remembered why his father had told him *never* to do that, and cried out in pain.

* * *

Secretary Spires was just nodding off when a gangly, out-of-breath guard came pelting into the secretary's elaborately decorative bedroom.

'M-murder,' he panted, almost bent double with exhaustion. 'M-murder, Mr Spires.'

The secretary, who hadn't been able to catch a wink since the viscount's kidnap two nights before, automatically leaped to his feet, knocking over his wash bowl in the process.

'Is it the viscount?' he said, staring around bleary-eyed. 'Have you found Lord Curfew?'

The guard shook his head.

'No, Mr Spires, it's definitely not the viscount,' the guard wheezed on. 'We found this fella wedged inside a wardrobe in one of the first-floor bedrooms.'

Spires heaved a slightly diluted sigh of relief, then sat back down on the bed, realised the magnitude of what he'd just been told, and leaped back up again.

'Do we have any idea who it is?'

The guard shrugged.

'I've never seen him before, Mr Spires, but the lads on the gate reckon it's the man who brings in all the vegetables.'

Spires' eyes widened, and watered.

'Fetch Enoch Dwellings,' he said. 'IMMEDIATELY.'

Eleven

Midnight fell on Dullitch like a drunken reveller tripping over his own shoelaces: hard and fast.

Deep below the palace, a subterranean tunnel intended solely for excrement suddenly acquired two extremely different sorts of filth.

'I don't believe this,' said Obegarde, plummeting into the river of muck from a dingy hatch in the tunnel roof. 'I thought you said you knew a "tried and trusted" way into the palace!'

'I do!' said Jimmy Quickstint, lithely snaking his way down from the hole. 'This is it!'

'Ha! You're not serious? Who in their right mind would even try this place, let alone trust it!'

'Er . . . are you going to whine all night, or are you actually interested in breaching the palace?'

'If you don't keep your mouth shut, I'll breach you.'

'Fine. Good luck finding your way out.'

Obegarde took a deep breath and counted to ten. Then he exhaled, very slowly.

'Shall I just show you the way in, then?' said Jimmy, noticing that the vampire's clenched fists had actually drawn blood from his palms.

'Yes, I would if I were you.'

'Righty ho . . . er . . . no problem.' He swung his arms as he walked. 'Hey, guess what, this afternoon I heard a vicious rumour that the viscount was kidnapped!'

'Really?'

'Yeah, straight up! What d'you reckon?'

'Me? I don't have a clue; but if you can get me into the palace I might at least be able to make an educated guess!'

'Ah . . . so he *has* been kidnapped, then?'

'Shut up, Jimmy. Just shut up.'

'Fine: well, we need to take a left here.'

The smell of sewage was now beyond belief. Obegarde fished in his pocket for a scrap of rag, and quickly covered his mouth and nose.

'What's that for?' Jimmy asked, perplexed.

The vampire stared at him for a moment.

'You're joking, right?'

'No, I'm serious – what's with the hanky?'

'The smell is unbelievable!'

Jimmy sniffed the air.

'What smell? I don't smell anything.'

'I'll assume that's a very bad attempt at humour.'

'No, really I don't; then again, I haven't exactly got a terrific sense of smell.'

'You don't say?'

The two men walked on in silence for a while, Jimmy stopping occasionally to check the map imprinted on his memory.

'Down here, I reckon,' he muttered, leading the vampire along a dank, foul-smelling tunnel that looked much like all the others they'd trawled through.

'How much further?' said Obegarde impatiently.

Jimmy shrugged.

'Hmm . . . difficult to say, really,' he mumbled. 'There's one particular landmark I'm looking for.'

'Down here? What is it, the statue of a tur—'

'Shh! I don't know what it is exactly, but I'll recognise it when I see it. OK?'

'It'll have to be, won't it?'

There was a moment of strained silence as Jimmy paused at the mouth of a four-way junction; went left, came back, went right, came back, then began to venture ahead.

Obegarde watched him carefully.

'You really don't have the slightest idea where you're leading us, do you?' he whispered.

'As a matter of fact, I do,' said Jimmy, turning to eye the vampire resentfully. 'Furthermore, I think if you go on ahead you will find a large, green and gold water pipe around the very next corner.'

Obegarde put his head on one side, then shoved Jimmy back against the wall and disappeared around the near bend. After a few seconds, he came striding back, rubbing his forehead.

'What happened?' Jimmy asked, a half-smile playing on his face. 'Are you all right?'

'No,' said Obegarde bitterly. 'I just whacked my skull on the large, green and gold water pipe THAT ISN'T BLOODY THERE.'

He snatched the gravedigger by his collar, hoisted him into the air and deposited him face-first into the muck.

'Now,' he said, stepping over the sopping-wet form and thrusting a finger under Jimmy's dripping nose. 'You better find the right tunnel fast. Otherwise, one of us is going to be having supper down here.'

Enoch Dwellings arrived at the palace confused, annoyed and in a hurry. On top of everything else, an obscure note from Obegarde, apologising for accidentally giving him a cat, had him unutterably bewildered. Could he have meant the stray that Wheredad had recently found in the bedroom?

Dwellings shook himself from his reverie. He couldn't

think about that *now*. Duty called . . . and it had certainly called *loudly* tonight.

Dwellings leaped up the main palace steps and was immediately ushered into a lobby room poorly decorated with torn drapes, tatty furniture, a great oak desk . . . and a battered corpse.

'When was it found?' Dwellings asked the nearest guard, throwing his coat over an armchair that looked grubby but was probably worth more than his house.

'*He* was found a short while ago, in a wardrobe in one of the bedrooms.'

Dwellings examined the man carefully, and nodded.

'Hmm . . .' he began. 'Beaten pretty badly . . . but no stab wounds; some signs of strangulation, though. I suppose he might have been poisoned, but I doubt it in the extreme. Who found him?'

One of a handful of guards that were dawdling around the door sheepishly raised a hand.

'I did, sir.'

'Was he hanging?'

'Sir?'

Dwellings rolled his eyes.

'Inside the wardrobe, man! Was he *hanging inside the wardrobe*?'

'Er . . . yeah, I fink so, sir.'

'You *think* so?'

'Yeah. I mean, I didn't akshully notice 'im at first . . .'

'How so?'

'Well, he was kinda propped up in one corner.'

'I see. Did he fall out on you?'

The guard shook his head.

'Not till I pushed 'im aside, no.'

'Pushed him aside?' Dwellings repeated, aghast. 'Why on Illmoor did you push this man aside?'

The guard shrugged.

'I needed to get at sumfing b'hind 'im.'

Dwellings drew in a breath.

'What was it you were trying to reach, exactly?'

'Coat hanger, sir. Why, is that 'mportant?'

'It might be.' Dwellings took a step back from the corpse, then produced his writing pad. 'So let me get this straight,' he began, scribbling furiously. 'You went into the bedroom, opened up the wardrobe and saw a dead man inside.'

''Sright.'

'So you pushed the dead man *aside* to get at the coat hanger, and he fell out of the wardrobe. It was *then* that you raised the alarm. Am I correct?'

'APSOLOOTLY, sir.'

'Very good, private. Thank you for your time.'

'I'm a sergeant, akshully, sir.'

Dwellings smiled.

'Are you really? Oh dear.'

'Excuse me. If I may interrupt . . .'

Secretary Spires entered the room to a flurry of salutes, and headed straight for Dwellings.

'You've had a good look, detective?' he said, indicating the corpse with a wave of his hand.

'Yes, thank you.'

'It's the vegetable delivery man, we believe.'

'Yes,' Dwellings agreed. 'Curiouser and curiouser.'

'So, are we forming a picture yet?' Spires asked, dismissing the guards and closing the door carefully behind them.

Dwellings shook his head.

'Not as such,' he admitted. 'But I am beginning to see the merest hint of an outline.'

'Oh good,' Spires said, taking a seat on one of the grand sofas and offering the detective a place beside him. 'Care to enlighten one less criminally-minded?'

Dwellings leaned back on the sofa, and pinched the bridge of his nose.

'I don't mind telling you, Mr Spires, that it's a tangled mess we have here.'

The secretary nodded.

'The fact is,' Dwellings went on, 'that *something* began the night before last with the kitchen's regular delivery of vegetables. The deliveryman drove the cart into the palace, but I'm absolutely *certain* that he didn't drive it out again. What I *think* happened was this: he hung around the palace for a few hours, talking to a succession of busy people, and then he came across what he thought was the cleaning crew.'

'You mean the men who arrived with the dustsheets?'

'Precisely: the men who are, I believe, a bunch of despicable, murdering kidnappers. Anyway, the deliveryman doesn't know this and, not having seen them before, he plagues them with questions and gets himself killed. An alternative theory is that the group had been watching the palace for some time, and knew about the deliveryman's routine. Anyway, back to the point: the kidnapping takes place and, in order to confuse the trail, they take *two* carts out of the city: the vegetable cart and their *own*. One contains the viscount, the other, we assume, is empty. This all takes time, as it is my belief that the group originate from around Crust . . .'

'And you believe this because . . . ?'

'Well, because of the two dead Crusters that turned up on the same vegetable cart this morning at eight o'clock.'

There was an awkward pause.

'How can it be the same cart?' said Spires, raising an eyebrow. 'That would mean they came back . . .'

Dwellings heaved an empty sigh.

'Well,' he said. 'I'm almost entirely convinced that they *did* return to the city . . . and are, in fact, still here. However, even if they *are*, finding them will be impossible: tracing their movements from the palace would be our best bet. I know, Mr Secretary, that it is a terrible and complicated mess, but I can assure you that I *am* on the case.'

Spires nodded, but somewhat despondently.

'You still have no explanation of the mechanics of the kidnapping?' he hazarded, listlessly.

'Actually, I do,' the detective admitted. 'I believe that the sleep, and the broken mirrors and windows, were all brought about by the death cry of the Jenacle banshee: it also backs up my theory about the kidnappers hailing from Crust, where such creatures are commonly bred. I suspect that a *separate* individual, possibly the most important member of the kidnapping team, crossed the rooftops of the city in order to get to the palace. I think it very likely that the poor Guard Marshal on duty at the North Gate tried to head him off. It would also explain why Curfew and the guard at the High Tower were unaffected by the cry: it seems almost certain that they were both wearing earplugs.'

'A marvellous set of deductions,' finished Spires, abruptly. 'In fact, Mr Dwellings, I only have one question remaining.'

'Which is?'

Spires took a deep breath.

'Do you plan on solving this case and *finding* the viscount before one – or worse – *both* of us are executed . . . ?'

'Of course!'

Enoch smiled nervously, bowed and quickly backed out of the room. When he got into the corridor beyond, he had to hold on to the wall for support: explanations made him weary ... and he really needed some sleep.

'Oh, here we go.'

Jimmy pointed left at what felt to Obegarde like the six millionth junction they'd come across, and gave a 'thumbs up' sign.

'I think this is it,' he confirmed, winking at the vampire and clicking his tongue. 'Told you I could get you into the palace, didn't I?'

They headed down the new tunnel, which ended rather abruptly in the form of a locked wooden door.

Jimmy waited for a few seconds. Then, when the vampire gave no hint of movement, he turned and motioned to him.

'What's that supposed to mean?' said Obegarde, dubiously.

Jimmy rolled his eyes.

'Aren't you going to kick it down?' he ventured.

'Kick what down? Oh, you mean this whacking great door blocking the passage? No, I'm not going to knock it down.'

'Why's that?'

'Because I'm a vampire and not a bloody cave troll, that's why.'

Jimmy's expression didn't change.

'You mean you can't knock this door down?' he hazarded.

'No.'

'What, really?'

'Really.'

'Damn, but you must be a wimp – I was even going to have a go at this one *myself.*'

Obegarde ignored the gravedigger's 'rolling up of sleeves' pantomime and gave the door an experimental barge with his shoulder. Nothing happened.

'Ah, I see what you're on about, now,' Jimmy said, leaning against the tunnel wall with his arms folded. 'There definitely wasn't much strength behind *that* assault.'

'Look,' Obegarde growled. 'I'm going to show you the true meaning of the word assault if you don't shut up.'

He took a few steps back, then ran up and charged into the door with all his might.

Still nothing.

'Why don't you vamp up?' Jimmy suggested.

Obegarde boggled at him.

'Why don't I *what*?'

'Vamp up.'

'What does that mean, for crying out loud?'

'You know,' Jimmy went on, making a monstrous face and gritting his teeth. 'That thing you all do, that hulking up thing where you go nuts and bite your own tongues off: I read about it.'

Obegarde shook his head in disbelief.

'And what good would biting my tongue off do me, exactly? Apart from making me unable to insult you for having such a stupid idea, that is. Any other suggestions?'

Jimmy thought for a moment, then shrugged.

'You could turn into a mist!'

'I can't do that: I'm only a *half*-vampire, remember? Us loftwings can't do mists: in fact, even rats and wolves give us problems. The only things we can turn into on a regular basis are bats and—'

'North Street?'

'No, I was going to say snakes.'

The gravedigger was momentarily speechless.

'Y-you?' he managed, eventually. '*You* can turn into a snake? Well, I'll be a werewolf's nephew: you kept that a bit quiet, didn't you?'

Obegarde shrugged.

'It's not the sort of thing you announce,' he said.

'That means you could get under the door!'

'I know.'

'Well, what are you waiting for?'

Obegarde looked up and down the tunnel, then pulled Jimmy closer to him.

'Listen, thief—'

'Gravedigger.'

'WHATEVER: just listen. If I want to turn into a snake, I have to excrete all my body waste first. Now, that means I need to find a quiet place somewhere to . . . relieve myself. Understand?'

Jimmy managed to suppress the smile that threatened to engulf his face.

'Completely,' he said. 'There's actually a cubby hole in the east wall about two tunnels back; looks just the ticket.'

'OK,' said Obegarde, searching the gravedigger's face for the merest hint of a grin. 'You keep watch: I'll be back shortly.'

'Need any help?'

'NONE. Just keep watch.'

'Loud and clear,' Jimmy whispered. 'You go and conduct your business, and you can trust me never to tell a soul.'

'Ha! I wouldn't trust *you* to unclog my pipes.'

'I thought you said you didn't need any help.'

'Very funny,' Obegarde called back. 'You know, one day that wit of yours is going to get you into a lot of trouble.'

You mean a lot MORE trouble, Jimmy thought bitterly, peering around at the tunnel walls. Then he saw the snake twisting and writhing through the water towards him.

'Blimey, Obegarde,' he said, under his breath. 'That was quick!'

The snake slid closer, hissing in the semi-darkness.

Jimmy jumped back from it.

'Hey, careful! You're after the door, not me, remember?'

The snake reared up, unveiling two halves of a dark, scaly hood, and darted for the gravedigger's throat.

Twelve

When Dwellings returned to his office, exhausted and completely out of breath, he found his unflappable assistant waiting for him. This was particularly annoying, as he'd left a detailed explanation of his thoughts on the desk, which he'd hoped the man would read.

'What do you want, Wheredad?' he demanded. 'It's two o'clock in the morning!'

'I'm so glad you're back, Enoch,' said the assistant, grimly, taking little notice of his employer's tone. 'I've had an idea.'

Dwellings yawned, his eyes heavy.

'Listen,' Wheredad ploughed on. 'What if the perpetrators of this crime used two carts—'

'We've already established that.'

'Yes, but what if they used *both* carts *inside* Dullitch . . . and both carts to get to and from the city at various times?'

'Go on . . .'

Wheredad smiled, brightly.

'Well, we know they used the one with the dustsheets, which is probably their own, but we've GOT the other cart: the one you say that they brought back this morning? Isn't there a chance that they took it to their hideout?'

'And?'

'AND if we've got the other cart, we can study the cart's tread . . .'

'Yes, I see where you're going,' said Dwellings, patiently. 'But it still doesn't bring us any closer to actually tracking them down, does it?'

'Maybe not,' said Wheredad, snapping his fingers. 'But *track* being the operative word, it might bring *someone else* a LOT closer.'

'Someone else? Closer to who? What *are* you babbling about?'

Wheredad drew himself up to his full impressive height and positively beamed.

'A tracker,' he said. 'If the cart leaves tracks, which it does, then all we need to do is hire a good tracker. I know the average Joe isn't going to recognise one cart tread from another, but a good tracker could do the job straight away. Am I right?'

Dwellings didn't smile straight away. Instead, it happened slowly, over the course of a few minutes.

'That, my friend,' he said, carefully, 'may be the most useful idea you've ever had.'

'I know! It's brilliant, isn't it!'

'Wait, though!' Dwellings held up an admonitory finger. 'Let's not get too carried away: we need to contact the palace to ensure they don't allow any carts through the tradesmen's entrance until after we've found a tracker: it'll be difficult enough to identify the right tracks without another five or ten to choose from.'

Wheredad, still beaming, shook his shaggy head.

'You're worrying over nothing, Enoch. I've *already* spoken to the palace guards and I've *already* had the side entrance sealed. All *we* need to worry about is finding the right man for the job.'

'Ha! We've got absolutely no worries there,' Dwellings exclaimed. 'I know the perfect candidate!'

The detective's suddenly animated expression gave his assistant a nasty feeling in the pit of his stomach.

'You don't mean . . .'

'Precisely, Wheredad.'

'But he's . . .'

'I know.'

'And he's . . .'

'That's right.'

'But he's not even . . .'

'Just accept it, Wheredad: Parsnip Daily is the only

117

tracker in the city who'll take on a task like this. Now, do you think I can get some sleep?'

Jimmy leaped back just in time to avoid the darting snake, which collided with the tunnel wall and splashed into the river of muck, quickly slithering beneath the surface.

Jimmy's mind froze with fear. Fortunately, his instinct for danger was already operating his limbs, so he immediately jumped up, took hold of the bar on the tunnel roof and swung his legs up at the same time. He'd just heaved himself from the water when the snake surfaced again, its wicked eyes glowing amber in the flickering shadows. Then it sank once again, and was gone . . .'

. . . just as a second snake emerged from around the bend in the tunnel. This one swam straight under the suspended form of Jimmy Quickstint before proceeding along the tunnel and slithering quickly under the door. There was a curious 'popping' noise from beyond the portal, then the unmistakable sound of a bolt sliding back, and finally Obegarde emerged, in human form, from the doorway.

'What're you doing up there?' he asked Jimmy, staring at him with a look of strange bewilderment.

Jimmy waited a few seconds, then lowered himself from the roof of the tunnel.

'Th-there was a snake,' he panted.

'I know that, you idiot! What did you think I was going to do, constrict you?'

The gravedigger shook his head.

'Not you,' he said. 'Another snake, just now, in the tunnel.'

Obegarde peered down at his feet.

'Are you sure?' he asked, kicking the murky waters around him, experimentally.

Jimmy nodded.

'I'm absolutely certain.'

'Fine, but, well, you've got to expect them, haven't you? I mean, this *is* a dark, dank sewer, after all!'

'Yeah,' said Jimmy, doubtfully. 'Mind you, this snake was weird. Its eyes looked kind of – you know – human.'

Obegarde shook his head.

'That's just snakes,' he muttered. 'They're all weird-looking things and they all freak people out: it's understandable, isn't it?'

'Yeah,' Jimmy whispered, looking dubiously into the dirty sewage water. 'Whatever you say, Obegarde, whatever you say . . .'

'C'mon,' the vampire prompted, disappearing behind the portal once again. 'Let's see where this forbidden passage leads us . . .'

Enoch Dwellings was trying to sleep. Having spent several minutes searching without success for a comfortable position on the mattress, he retired to the floor in the

desperate hope that Wheredad's constant stomping
around downstairs would be drowned out by the noise of
the seven million woodlice that held a nightly soccer
match on the underside of the floorboards.

It really was going to be one of those nights.

The tunnel in which Jimmy and Obegarde now found
themselves was considerably lighter than the ones they'd
passed through in order to get to it. There were also
torches on brackets and handrails fastened to the walls,
and Obegarde felt sure that the tunnel was beginning
to ascend.

'It's getting clearer,' said Jimmy, peering up ahead.

'What, the tunnel?' Obegarde ventured, trying to see
around Jimmy's head.

'No, not the tunnel; the *water*. There's not so much
. . . you know . . . *stuff* in it.'

'Yeah, I noticed that. Do you think we're nearly there?'

The gravedigger nodded.

'Told you I knew my way about down here, didn't I?'

'Yes, all right! Don't go on about it!'

Jimmy muttered something under his breath.

After a few more minutes of quiet progress which
took them around several bends, they arrived at the
foot of a very steep, very ancient-looking staircase. Jimmy
peered up into the gloom.

'This is it,' he said. 'You follow these stairs, and they'll
take you straight to the palace wine cellar.'

Obegarde nodded.

'Right,' said Jimmy. 'That's me just about done, then. Good luck, eh!'

He turned to leave and suddenly felt the vampire's icy grip on his neck.

'And where do you think *you're* going?' Obegarde challenged, one eyebrow raised quizzically.

'I – er – I've done what you wanted me to do!'

Obegarde shook his head.

'I've changed my mind,' he muttered. 'You're coming in with me . . .'

'Am I hell!'

'Not yet, but you *will* visit hell if you try to get out of accompanying me into the palace.'

Jimmy rolled his eyes.

'Oh, why can't you go in there on your own? Are you some sort of big, one-fanged coward?'

'I'll pretend I didn't hear that, Jimmy. Now just move yourself, will you?'

The gravedigger swore a few times under his breath, then began to stomp angrily up the stairs, deliberately splashing puddles of filthy water behind him.

'I swear,' Obegarde mumbled, 'that you are one of the most annoying people I've ever had the misfortune to meet.'

'Ha! You and me both, Overbite.'

'You do realise that I could smack you through the wall of this tunnel with little or no physical effort?'

'Yeah, you and half the folk in this city. You're nothing special for being able to beat up li'l Jimmy. Besides, you're not *that* tough: Groan Teethgrit'd put you down like a skittle.'

'Groan Teethgrit? What, the barbarian with a bacon sandwich for a brain? Oh yes, I think I've heard of him.'

'Ha! You wouldn't say that if he was standing here: you'd turn and run like a badger with a bum full o' gunpowder.'

'No I wouldn't.'

'Sure, Obegarde; whatever you sa—'

Jimmy suddenly stopped dead in his tracks, and Obegarde knocked into him.

'What's wrong?' the vampire said, stepping back. 'Can you see something?'

Jimmy nodded, motioned up ahead.

'There's someone there,' he whispered, moving aside so that the vampire could see.

Obegarde glimpsed the shadowy figure at the top of the stairs.

'I thought you said that none of the guards knew about this place!' he moaned.

'I did,' said Jimmy, concern in his voice. 'And that isn't a guard; it's too small.'

Obegarde nodded in the half dark.

'Well, if it's not a guard, then what – I mean *who* – is it?'

'I think you were closer when you said "what",' Jimmy

intoned, 'because I think that bloke up there is the same one who attacked me in the sewer tunnel.'

Obegarde frowned.

'I thought you were attacked by a snake back there?' he said.

'I was,' said Jimmy, stroking his chin thoughtfully. 'But I've got a really strong feeling it might have been a shapeshifter; its eyes had a kind of weird glow to 'em.'

'Oh, great.'

Jimmy took a deep breath.

'You reckon you can handle a shapeshifter?' he ventured.

Obegarde shrugged.

'I don't see why not . . .'

'Good job, because he's coming down . . . FAST.'

Jimmy leaped back as the spindly stranger came speeding towards them, leaping two or three steps at a time in a sort of diagonal pounce.

Obegarde didn't move; instead he put both hands firmly on the rails either side of him and gripped with all his might.

When the creature, who resembled a particularly anaemic human, neared the duo on the stairs, it changed tactics and leaped on to one of the side rails, sliding towards them in a crouched position.

Obegarde knew instinctively that it was going to try to leap over them; something about the way it moved insinuated that it had achieved its goal, and that now its only priority was to leave as quickly as possible. The conundrum was whether or not to try to stop it . . .

Unfortunately, Obegarde didn't have time to decide.

The shapeshifter – for its eyes betrayed it as such – leaped into the air and somersaulted over the vampire, drawing a needle-thin blade in the process.

Obegarde quickly spun around and snatched hold of the creature's shoulder, reeling when it turned and slashed a vicious wound across his mouth.

The vampire staggered back, clutching at his bleeding lips, and struck out with his foot instead. He caught the creature squarely in the chest, a move which forced it to emit a terrible hiss as it tumbled backwards.

Jimmy dived out of the way as it rolled and plummeted down the remaining steps. When it landed in a puddle at the foot of the flight, it scowled up at them and a look of intense hatred illuminated its bulbous red eyes.

'Get yooouu,' it hissed. 'Get you gooood.'

Then it morphed back into snake-form and slithered beneath the water.

Jimmy watched to make sure it was gone before hurrying up to Obegarde, who was still clutching his face and moaning terribly.

'Here,' Jimmy said, producing a silk handkerchief and passing it to the vampire. 'You better clean yourself up; you can't sneak into the palace dripping blood, can you?'

Obegarde stared at the handkerchief.

'Is that stolen?' he asked.

'Why? Is it yours?'

'No.'

'What're you worried about, then?'

The vampire snatched the handkerchief and pressed it to his mouth, muttering obscenities under his breath. Eventually, he managed to ebb the flow of blood.

'What do you think a thing like *that* was doing in the palace?' he managed, still dabbing half-heartedly at the wound.

'Who knows?' said Jimmy, shivering at the thought. 'Maybe he lives down here or something.'

Obegarde shook his head.

'No,' he said. 'Definitely not; he came for something . . .'

'. . . or someone,' Jimmy finished. 'Maybe it's the secretary's turn to get kidnapped. Shall we find out?'

'No.'

'What?'

The vampire dabbed at his face once more.

'I've changed my mind,' he said. 'I'm not going into the palace . . .'

'But . . . why? We've come all this way, now; we have to go in!'

Obegarde shook his head.

'I only wanted to get inside so I could dig up some more information on the viscount's disappearance!'

'And?'

'And now I've got it! I can *use* this information to get Dwellings to tell me everything he knows about the case!'

Jimmy's features creased into a frown.

'Who's Dwellings?' he asked, scratching his head.

'Enoch Dwellings; the detective who's handling the whole affair.'

'Ah ... right. So what you're basically saying is that I've just trawled through half of Illmoor's snake-infested sewer system for bugger all.'

Obegarde put his head on one side.

'Not entirely for nothing,' he said, reaching down and snatching a small object from the floor of the tunnel. He held it up between thumb and forefinger. 'Well, what do you know?' he muttered, pushing the object under Jimmy's nose. 'If it isn't a ring with the royal seal on it!'

Jimmy studied the ring, and gulped. 'Do you think our slithery friend dropped it in the scuffle?'

'I'd put money on it.'

'Can I have it, then?'

Obegarde looked up at the gravedigger, and burst out laughing.

'What?' Jimmy demanded, his thin brows knitting in annoyance. 'What are you laughing at?'

'YOU!'

'What did I say?'

Obegarde slipped the ring on to his finger.

'This is valuable evidence,' he said, tapping the find with his thumb. 'Why would I ever want to give it to you?'

'Er ... maybe because you owe me for risking countless dangers in helping you find the secret entrance to the palace?'

Obegarde sniffed, shook his head.

'I already gave you your fifty crowns,' he said, turning around and trudging off towards the vast tunnel network. 'Consider yourself paid.'

'But . . .'

'Hey, if you're *that* hard-up, you could always sneak into the wine cellar and take your chances with the palace guards . . .'

'Thanks, Obegarde: thanks a lot.'

Jimmy cursed all vampires under his breath, and stomped off after him.

Thirteen

It was a bright and breezy morning in Dullitch, and the streets were already heaving with (largely resentful) life.

'Look, I know you didn't get much sleep last night, Enoch,' said Wheredad, hurrying to keep up with the detective, who hadn't said a word during breakfast. 'But you really can't hire Parsnip Daily: not for a job as important and delicate as this!'

'Don't be ridiculous, man!' Dwellings snapped. 'He's perfect for the task! And, incidentally, the only reason I couldn't sleep last night, apart from the late call-out, was because you were smashing about downstairs with your size fifteens. *And* you let me leave the office this morning without my coat . . .'

'I said I was sorry.'

'It's not good enough; it really isn't.'

'But what about Daily? The man's a thief, Enoch!'

'AND?'

'*And* – AND he's got that weird mental thing where he can't remember anything for more than a few seconds!'

'So?'

'So what good is a tracker with no memory and a tendency to go rooting through your pockets in the middle of an investigation?'

Dwellings made no attempt to slow down.

'You're quite right, my friend. That's why we'll have to watch him carefully if he agrees to come. Besides, the memory thing is strange; it doesn't affect him *all* the time, and if his mind is properly focused, it doesn't affect him *at all*. He's just the ideal person to ask . . .'

'Oh, do we *have* to, Enoch?'

'*We* don't, Wheredad; *I* do.'

'And the stealing? How do you propose to get round that?'

'He does NOT steal; he simply borrows things and then *forgets* that they belong to other people.'

'That's the same thing!'

'No no no! It's not the same at all. Look, say I want to buy a lamp, right? I go along to the Market Place to pick one up, find a little beauty and then, as I'm holding it, I *forget* that I went out looking for a lamp.'

'So what explanation would you give yourself for the lamp you're holding in your hands?'

'No explanation at all. I'd simply think that it was mine to begin with.'

Wheredad hurried to keep up.

'But that's ridiculous, Enoch! It's no wonder he's been in and out of prison so much; the man's a menace to society.'

'That's as may be, Wheredad, but he's also a damn good tracker. Now *do* try to keep up: once I've fetched my coat from the office, we're going to call in at the Ferret, the Furrier's Arms and Mo Jangly's Gambling Pit. We need to find Parsnip soon.'

'Do you know what he looks like?'

'Haven't got a clue, but his reputation precedes him. Besides, *everyone* knows at least two people who know him: we'll find the fellow somehow.'

Arriving back at his office, Dwellings suddenly stopped short. Standing at the top of the stairs was the vampire's assistant.

'What do you want?' he said, gruffly, pushing Wheredad back when the assistant walked into him.

Lusa hugged her arms for warmth.

'I need to speak with you,' she said. 'It's quite important.'

Obegarde woke up smelling of sewerage. He lifted the lid of his coffin and rolled out, struggling awkwardly to his feet.

'Lusa!' he yelled, looking around for a teacup and finding his overcoat instead. 'Lusa! Where are you, for crying out loud?'

'Thank you for telling me all that,' said Dwellings, passing a plate of cup cakes across to his guest. 'It must have taken a great deal of courage.'

Lusa nodded.

'I thought you should know; it wouldn't be fair, otherwise. But, like I just explained, he *is* my dad and I wouldn't want him to get into trouble because of me . . .'

'You did the right thing,' said Dwellings, grinning awkwardly as the girl chose a cake from the selection on offer. 'You'll have another tea, I assume?'

Lusa shook her head.

'I shouldn't really,' she said. 'I'd like to be back in the office when he returns.'

'Oh nonsense!' said Dwellings, with sudden gusto. 'One small cup won't delay you by much! Wheredad; fetch another pot of tea, there's a good chap.'

The burly assistant quickly detached himself from the corner he'd been silently rooted in since they had returned, and busied himself in the kitchen. It wasn't often that Enoch Dwellings enjoyed the company of young women, so Wheredad didn't really know what to do with himself; he felt awkward, useless and, above all, visible. Moreover, he was worried . . . if Dwellings got himself a girlfriend before *he* did, he was quite sure he'd never hear the last of it . . .

Like many loftwings, Obegarde was not a morning person. Having managed to claw his way blearily into the light, he headed clumsily for the office of Enoch Dwellings, and was rather taken aback when his daughter answered the door.

'What are you doing here?' he snapped.

Lusa put a hand over his mouth.

'Never mind that,' she said. 'What in the name of Yowler do you smell like?'

Obegarde looked down at his stinking clothes, as if noticing them for the first time.

'I've been in the sewer,' he explained.

'You don't say?'

'Look, you haven't told him anything, have you?'

'Well, we had quite a nice chat, and he knows I'm your daughter . . .'

'Fantastic.'

'Oh, it's OK; he's quite nice when you get to know him.'

Obegarde cracked his knuckles.

'You didn't say anything about the *other* thing, did you?'

Lusa smiled sweetly, and stepped aside to allow her father entrance.

Fourteen

Another nightmare . . .

. . . and Curfew awoke for the second time, screaming. For a few seconds, it was an involuntary action, but he soon realised that he was screaming through choice, not pain, and he began to draw in his cries. His temple throbbed: he couldn't tell whether he'd been unconscious for minutes, hours or days.

His eyelids flickered . . .

. . . and the nightmare returned, in vivid detail. It was identical to the one he'd had before: slithering darkness and terrible pits. He fought it this time, and awoke, cold . . .

The cell was empty.

Curfew stared at his surroundings. One thing was certain: the group that had kidnapped him – assuming it *was* a group – counted at least one enchanter among its number: no nightmare felt *that* vivid without magic being involved somewhere ... even Duke Threefold's skeleton had disappeared: another dream-induced illusion from his cruel and twisted captors, no doubt.

Curfew checked his body for wounds, but found no sign of even superficial damage. He smelled though, and his clothes had turned from finely fitting garments into sweat-drenched rags.

However, it appeared that he *was* now unchained, and his bonds and gags had disappeared. Had they, in fact, existed at all? A wall of frustrated confusion was building up inside him.

Struggling to his feet, Curfew staggered over to the heavy oak door and attempted to pull himself up using the thick bars on the door's small hatch.

'H-help me,' he cried, to the accompaniment of a sudden eruption of cruel laughter. He turned around and slumped against the door, allowing himself to slide despairingly to the ground. The laughter stopped, and silence reigned for a time. Then came the drip ...

... drip ...

... drip from the moss-covered roof of the cell.

'Somebody help me,' he managed. This time, the words were spoken softly, to himself ...

... and they were answered.

At first, Curfew thought that he had imagined the sound; a kind of tiny, far-off echo. However, as he moved around the wall, listening desperately for any sign that he'd been right, the sound became clearer.

Having reached the far corner of the cell, he stopped, crouched and listened again.

'. . . ere?'

There was no mistaking it this time; the voice was there; fractured and distant, but *there*.

Curfew reached down and scraped at the wall; his fingers worked away several thick patches of moss and a clump of grass that was concealing the outflow of a small drainage pipe.

The viscount lay flat on his stomach, cupped a hand over his mouth and called into the pipe:

'Is there somebody else there?'

There was a moment of silence, then a voice replied: 'What, you mean apart from me?'

Curfew started, reeled back from the pipe.

'Who is this?' he called.

'Who is *this*?'

'I am Viscount Curfew, Lord of Dullitch. And *this* is?' Nothing.

Curfew cleared his throat. 'And this is?' he repeated.

'Yes?' came the voice. 'I'm waiting . . .'

'For what?'

'For you to introduce me!'

Curfew frowned.

'To who?'

'To your cell-mate!'

'I don't have one; I'm on my own in here!'

'But you said "and this is . . ." so I thought there were
two of you in there!'

'Oh . . . right, well there isn't.' Curfew rolled his eyes;
he'd obviously stumbled upon an absolute lunatic.
'Anyway, as I was saying, I am Viscount Curfew . . .
AND THIS IS?'

'Are you schizophrenic or something?'

'NO, DAMN IT! I'm just trying to find out who YOU
ARE! Is it really that difficult to tell me your name?'

There was a momentary pause, before the voice
returned.

'I'm Innesell,' it said.

Curfew muttered something under his breath.

'What was that?' enquired the voice.

'I said: THAT'S FAIRLY OBVIOUS,' Curfew called.
'But what is your name?'

'I just told you; my name's Innesell! Look, I know it's
kind of a funny handle in my present situation, but even
so, a name is what it is: there's nothing I can do about
it.'

'Your name is Innesell?'

'Yes.'

'Really?'

'YES. I'd have to be right on the verge of madness to
make something like *that* up, wouldn't I?'

'Hmm . . . I suppose so.' Curfew thought for a moment. 'What do you do, Innesell? Are you a member of the nobility?' He asked the last question very doubtfully.

'No,' came the expected reply. Then: 'I'm a baker's assistant. Why did you think I was a noble?'

Curfew brought his mouth closer to the pipe.

'I didn't; but you reacted strangely when I told you I was the Lord of Dullitch, so I thought you might be another noble.'

'I didn't react at all!'

'That's what I mean; people tend to gasp when I'm announced.'

'Oh right. Sorry; it's just that I knew you were down here; I've heard them talking about you.'

'Really? Who are *they*? What did they say?'

'Nothin' much; just said you were one hell of a swordfighter. Hey, are you *really* Viscount Curfew?'

'Yes.'

'*THE* Viscount Curfew?'

'Uhuh.'

'*Wicked* Viscount Curfew?'

'Ye— eh? What do you mean, "Wicked"? I'm not that bad!'

'From what I hear, you're an absolute nightma—'

'Yes, well, *anyway* . . . how did *you* end up down here?'

There was a brief pause in the conversation.

'Well?' the viscount prompted. 'What happened to you?'

'Forget it, lordy; 'sa long story.'

Curfew sighed.

'That doesn't matter,' he said. 'If there's one thing it looks like we've both got a lot of, it's time . . .'

There was another pregnant pause.

'Well, if I'm lucky I suppose *I* may have,' mumbled the voice, uncertainly. 'But unless there's more than one Viscount Curfew down here, I'm pretty sure they're planning to kill *you* at midnight.'

Fifteen

'All I'm saying,' Obegarde started, 'is that if we pool our resources, we stand a better chance of getting to the bottom of this . . .'

'Ha!' Dwellings exclaimed. 'And I suppose us *pooling* our resources involves *us* telling *you* everything we know, while you tell us the bundles of nothing *you've* managed to find out?'

'Hey! I've got vital infor—'

'Nonsense! How *could* you know something that I don't – I'm your *source*, aren't I?'

Obegarde stared at his feet for a second, then at his daughter and, finally, back to the detective.

'She told you, didn't she?' he said.

'You mean about the sneaking into my office and stealing all my cases? Oh yes, yes she did.'

'Are you angry?'

'Oh no, not at all. In fact, we're over the moon about it, aren't we, Wheredad?'

The big assistant glared at Obegarde and muttered his disapproval.

'Look,' said the vampire, his pale face beginning to flush. 'I'm sure we can work something out . . . ?'

'That all depends,' said Dwellings, casually. 'First, I want to know anything you *think* you've found out about the viscount's kidnapping – don't even pretend you didn't know about it – and then, I'd like to ask your daughter out on a date.'

Obegarde and Wheredad turned startled stares upon Dwellings, but their combined shock was as nothing to the look on Lusa's face.

'He's not my keeper!' she said, exasperated. 'Couldn't you have just asked me yourself?'

The detective shook his head.

'Less embarrassing this way round,' he said.

'For who?'

'For you – I mean, me; well, both of us! Anyway, what's the answer?'

Obegarde shrugged.

'I suppose—'

'NO!' Lusa cut in.

Dwellings swallowed a few times, then shook his head.

'No?' he said, his brow creased. 'That's your answer? No?'

Lusa folded her arms. 'You heard me.'

'But, why? What's wrong with me?'

'Nothing particularly, I just don't like you very much.'

'Oh.'

The silence hung in the air like poison, filling everyone with a sudden, intense need to study the walls.

'Right,' said Dwellings, now so red that his face resembled a beetroot. He turned back to Obegarde. 'What do you know about the case?'

The vampire clenched his fists, digging his long fingernails into his palm to stop himself laughing.

'I tried to sneak into the palace,' he said.

'And?' prompted Dwellings, ignoring the combined stares of the others.

'And I wasn't the only one. There was a shapeshifter in the sewers; he got in way ahead of us and stole—'

'I knew it! I just knew that one of them came back! A shapeshifter, you say?'

'Yes, he stole—'

'What kind?'

'A snake, but—'

'At least now we know the sort of scum that we're up against.'

'Yes,' said Obegarde, patiently. 'But if you'd just let me fin—'

'This doesn't fit,' said Dwellings, rubbing his chin,

thoughtfully. 'In fact, it makes everything much more complicated!'

'Well, that's why you should let me help you . . .'

'You? After what you've done? Ha! Forget it!'

Before the vampire could protest, Dwellings spun around and marched determinedly from the room, Wheredad trailing after him like an obedient bloodhound.

'Shame,' said Obegarde, turning to his daughter with a devilish grin on his face. He winked at her. 'I didn't get a chance to tell him about the ring I found in the sewers.'

Part Three

The Tracker

Lunchtime found Enoch Dwellings and his bumbling assistant stalking through a narrow street in downtown Dullitch.

'Nice of him to give us some information, though,' Wheredad reflected.

'Ha! He didn't have a choice.'

'You think you could've forced him to tell you things if he didn't want to?'

'Hmm ... frankly, yes. I've handled a good few vampires in my time. Don't you remember the one that was infesting Karuim's Church?'

'That was a bat, Enoch.'

'Ha! It still drank blood, didn't it?'

'Er . . . well, I don't know about that, but it certainly gave people a nasty bite.'

They walked in silence for a while.

'So where else is the *great* Parsnip Daily supposed to hang out?' Wheredad enquired, stepping around two ogres who'd already parted for Dwellings and didn't look like they were ready to repeat the courtesy. 'I mean, we've already searched the Ferret and Furrier's. Where else is there?'

'Mo Jangly's Gambling Pit,' the detective replied. 'But I'm postponing the search for Parsnip; there's somebody else I want to talk to first; somebody who always knows the goings-on in Dullitch and never fails to give 'em to me straight.'

'Oh?' said Wheredad, feigning ignorance. 'Who's that, then?'

'Stoater. I really don't know why we didn't go to him first: you know he sees *everything*.'

'I'll never understand why you don't just call him *the matchstick man*; I mean, it's not like there's another one in Dullitch . . .'

'I call him Stoater for the same reason that I call *you* Wheredad; it's his name. Besides, you're only bringing up the subject because you can't stand the fellow.'

'Nobody can, Enoch! He's an obnoxious little creep.'

Dwellings slowed a little, and turned to his colleague.

'It's not his fault he got cursed: he used to be—'

'Oh please: I've heard the story a thousand times!'

'Tell me, Wheredad, is there anybody in this city that you actually like?'

'Hmm . . . does—'

'. . . your mother count? No, she doesn't. I'm talking about *other people*.'

Wheredad muttered something under his breath and the two men walked in silence for a time. Eventually, they arrived at Dwellings' intended destination.

Thicket Alley, reputedly the most enchanted piece of land in Dullitch, was a complete mystery to Wheredad and, despite the amount of times Dwellings went there to consult his 'Eye on the Street', Wheredad could never find the place alone. He strongly suspected that the alley didn't stay in one place, though Dwellings always vehemently denied the suggestion.

He hurried to keep up with the detective, who had stopped some ten metres ahead and crouched down on his haunches.

Dwellings glanced back over his shoulder and motioned to his assistant to approach silently. Wheredad obliged.

The detective then sat, cross-legged, beside the mouth of a short, horizontal length of drainpipe, and knocked several times on the pipe itself.

'Stoater.'

Silence.

A second knock followed, louder this time.

'Stoater; are you in? It's me, Enoch.'

Still nothing.

Dwellings rolled his eyes, and brought his mouth level with the drainpipe opening.

'Listen, Stoater, I know you're in there, and if you don't come out this instant, I'm going to wee into the other end of the pipe.'

There was still no sign of movement from the pipe, but a little voice, high-pitched and clearly audible, said: 'You wouldn't dare.'

'Let's see, shall we?' said Dwellings, reaching into his pocket for a flask of tea. Unscrewing the cap, he poured a measure of milky liquid into the far end of the pipe . . .

. . . and a matchstick hurried out of the opposite end. It looked like any one of a million matchsticks available in small packets all over the city, with one noticeable difference: it had a tiny human face where the match-head should have been.

It looked livid.

'Eewugh! That's sick, that is. What the hell's wrong with you people? Isn't it bad enough that I was changed into this? I used to be—'

'A blacksmith. Yes, Stoater, we *know*.'

'Well, then . . . a little respect wouldn't go amiss. I could still give you a nasty burn, if I came at you from the right angle.'

'Of course you could.'

Dwellings secreted the flask about his person, and grinned down at the matchstick man.

'We need some help, Stoats.'

The matchstick man made a face.

'I've told you before, Enoch, I can't get you a girlfriend. You have to do these things for yourself.'

Dwellings' face turned red, then proceeded through black and purple before any pink patches re-emerged.

'I don't need a girlfriend,' he snapped.

'Hmm . . . well, *you* might not, but *I've* got a date in twenty minutes, so make it quick . . .'

Dwellings boggled at the creature.

'You? *You* have a date? What with, a roll-up?'

'Hey, don't insult me, *Dwellings*, I still have human thoughts, you know. As far as women are concerned, I look for the same thing you do . . .'

'A pulse?' Wheredad ventured.

Stoater erupted in squeals of laughter, but Dwellings glared at his assistant.

'Can we get back to the matter in hand?' he snapped, returning his gaze to the matchstick man. 'Listen, we need to know the word on the street.'

'Nah. Bog off!' said Stoater, angrily shaking a tiny pink stub at the detective. 'Who do think you are, Dwellings? You come down here with your fat monkey, knock seven bells out o' my pipe, you try to flush me out by widdling into my kitchen and then you insult me? Give me one good reason why I should tell you anything?'

Dwellings folded his arms and thought for a moment.

'I think you should tell me all you can,' he said, pursing his lips. 'Because I really feel like a cigarette right now and, not being a regular smoker, I don't have a tinderbox with me.'

'Oh, death threats now, is it?' said Stoater, gloomily. 'Nice. Always pick on the little guy, eh?'

'SO TELL ME!' Dwellings snapped.

'No!' The matchstick man shook his head. 'I really don't see why I should. After all, I told you about that business with the three whippets, didn't I? And what about that cartload of dwarves that dished into the river last summer; who was it told you the actual address of the nutter that cut the reins? And I ask you, what do I get for my trouble? Half a ruddy drainpipe to live in . . . and two dried biscuits from your tea cupboard.'

Dwellings shook his head.

'That wasn't enough?'

Stoater shrugged. 'Well, it's not exactly a win at the races, is it?'

'Look, just help us this one last time,' said Wheredad, who really despised the matchstick man for the constant abuse he and Dwellings had suffered each time they called at Thicket Alley. 'And then we promise never to call on you again.'

'Yes,' said Dwellings, keeping both fingers tightly crossed behind his back. 'And you can have another biscuit from the tea cupboard?'

'Oh, please, give me a break with the biscuits, will

you? I've still got half of the last one you gave me, and that's with two platefuls at every meal.'

'Look, you little woodchip, are you going to help us or not?'

'I might. What is it you want to know? You trying to find out who took out Marble Cole?'

'No.'

'You're after the gang that did Denbreaker the Half-ogre?'

'NO! We want to know—'

'Who kidnapped Viscount Curfew?'

Wheredad and Dwellings exchanged a significant glance before the detective indicated the accuracy of the guess.

'Thought so,' said Stoater, arrogantly. 'All that other stuff, I was just playin' with ya.'

'So,' Wheredad prompted, cracking his knuckles and fighting the urge to grab the little beast and strike him off the brickwork, 'who *did* kidnap the viscount?'

'Dunno,' the matchstick man admitted, but Dwellings smiled because he recognised Stoater's usual tendency to pause before the floodgates opened. 'Out of towners, though, and they def'nitely weren't takin' no chances. Three of 'em came in on a cart; two shapeshifters an' a rogue of some sort. They split up at the North Gate and the shifters continued in the cart while the rogue scaled the walls and came in over the rooftops. He carried a Jenacle banshee in a box: I know it was a Jenacle because

a tabby mate of mine saw him stabbing it in the palace kitchens, then a ferret I used to play cards with found the body in a dustbin near Widdlers Alley. Anyway, I'm gettin' off the point: word has it that a Guard Marshal on the outer wall spotted the rogue an' darted 'cross the city in order to try to cut him down. Unfortunately, he had no hope: the bloke was a real pro. The group did the dirty, nabbed Curfew and left in two carts, sometime after ten: a crow that I know on the palace roof reckons they put Curfew in the vegetable cart 'cause the gate guards're familiar with it and wouldn't check. They needn't have worried, though: the gate guards were gamblin' and no one stopped 'em anyway. Apparently, one of the shapeshifters came back this morning, dumped the vegetable cart and disappeared. Then a cockroach mate o' mine saw him steal a horse on Market Street: he prob'ly left the city on it.'

'Hang on a minute,' Dwellings interjected. 'I'm trying to find out what happened to that vegetable cart on the night of the kidnapping, after the group had left the city: I'm assuming they dumped it once they were beyond the walls?'

Stoater scratched himself, chipping off a tiny splinter in the process.

'Doubt it: a fox I know on the road to Crust told a cursed sparrow who used to be one of my regulars that he saw a vegetable cart haring through the Gleaming Mountains at one hell of a speed.'

'And after that?'

'Not a thing: sorry.'

Dwellings smiled up at Wheredad before returning his attention to the matchstick man.

'Anything else, Stoater?'

'Er . . . well, it was def'nitely a well-planned job, but rumour has it that the three of 'em came from somewhere up north. Funny thing is, they would have to o' been here for a few days to do a decent scout of the palace, but they definitely didn't stay in the city: must've gone for a place outside the walls.'

'That everything?'

'Yep.'

Dwellings nodded, beside himself with awe at the little matchstick man's unrivalled knowledge of city activity.

'I don't suppose . . .' he began, then hesitated.

'What?' said Stoater.

'Well, we're looking for a tracker called Parsnip Daily. We know the sort of places he hangs out, but we don't know what he—'

'Short, scruffy, silly hat with weeds growin' out of it. You can't miss him, though you *will* if you don't get to Jangly's Pit pretty sharpish; he usually calls it a day 'bout now,'

Dwellings grinned.

'Thank you once again, Stoater. I don't know *how* you do it . . .'

'Easy,' came the screechy reply. 'The trick is to talk to everyone, even if they don't seem keen to talk back. Take rats, for example; rats get everywhere and see everything, but does anyone think of asking 'em for information? Do they heck as like. If someone had just *talked* to those fellas during the Ratastrophe, a whole lot of fuss could've been avoided. I'm serious; if I had half a crown for every rat that's seen a murder, I'd be, what, six or seven crowns poorer than I am now?'

Wheredad squinted at the matchstick man as he tried to work this out, but Dwellings was already making his way back to the mouth of the alley.

'They made a fatal mistake,' the detective was saying to himself, when his big assistant drew level with him.

'Mmm?'

Dwellings grinned.

'The idiots should've switched carts again outside the city, and dumped the vegetable cart! Instead of that, they take it to their hideout and then BRING IT BACK to us! All we need to do is track the wheel-tread!'

'Er ... yes,' Wheredad managed. 'Isn't that what I said earlier?'

Two

Mo Jangly's Gambling Pit was a hot and sweaty hive of swift, underhanded activity.

Parsnip Daily stood at the wall-bar, watching the two men on the balcony of the pit watching the no-one-is-that-lucky gnome at the fortune tables. As soon as they spotted what *he'd* spotted – the foot pedal and the tiny mirrors on both toecaps – the afternoon would become a lot more interesting.

Parsnip lit a fat cigar, then remembered he'd found the thing on the floor of the pit and promptly coughed half his lungs up.

'You shouldn't smoke,' advised a passing stranger.

'I don't,' Daily called after him. He looked down at

the lighted stick in his hands; only the gods knew where he'd found it.

He sighed deeply, and stubbed the cigar out on the surface of a nearby table. That was the problem when you suffered memory loss and blackouts, you couldn't . . . you couldn't . . .

Parsnip Daily shook himself from his reverie, and returned his attention to the man with the donkey in the corner of the room. Hmm . . . had he been watching a man with a donkey?

When someone tapped Parsnip on the shoulder, he nearly jumped out of his skin.

Enoch Dwellings emerged from the smoke.

'Parsnip Daily?' he ventured.

Parsnip looked both ways before answering.

'Might be,' he said, slyly.

'Look, you either are or you aren't: it's a definite answer I'm after.'

'OK,' said Parsnip, evenly. 'Then I *definitely* might be. What do you want?'

'I need you to track someone for me.'

There was a moment of hesitation.

'Why me?'

'Because you're the best tracker in the city.'

'Am I?'

'You don't KNOW?'

'Well, no, I didn't, but then I've got this problem, you see . . .'

Recognition suddenly dawned, and Dwellings smiled knowingly.

'Ah, yes: I know all about your . . . er . . . your memory thing.'

'What memory thing?'

'You know; the stuff about your not remembering who you are, where you've just been . . .'

'Am I like that, then?' Parsnip sniffed the air, doubtfully. 'I thought I just suffered the odd . . . er . . .'

Dwellings waited a few moments, then said: 'Lapse?'

'Yeah, that's it. The odd . . . er . . .'

'Lapse?'

'Yes, got it in one.'

'No, Mr Daily. You have a *serious* memory problem; one that is as annoying as it is unfortunate.'

'Well, fine, but I reckon you're totally wrong about that . . .'

'Wrong about what?'

'Er . . .'

'Exactly.'

There was a pause.

'Well, if I really have got a memory problem,' the tracker continued, 'then how come I remember you from a few minutes ago?'

Dwellings smiled.

'You do?'

'I do what?'

'Remember me?'

'OK.'

'What do you mean "OK"?'

'I mean OK, I'll try to remember you.'

'No! Look...'

The detective rolled his eyes, and took one of his regularly necessary deep breaths.

'I'm going to start again, Parsnip,' he began. 'And I want you to listen very carefully...'

'Why should I?' said the tracker. 'Have we met?'

Dwellings briefly toyed with the notion of committing suicide, then thought better of it and tried again: 'How do you normally remember things?'

'I don't,' said Parsnip, decisively. 'I forget them.'

'I *know* that, but what about the *big* things, like where you live and what your name is, etc.?'

'Oh, I write all that stuff down.'

'Thank goodness,' said Dwellings, fighting mental exhaustion. 'Do you think you could write down everything I'm about to say?'

Parsnip nodded and reached into his coat, producing a thin stick of lead and a grubby old notebook.

'Right,' he muttered. 'Go ahead.'

'OK, you ready?'

'Yes.'

'I, Enoch Dwellings, need you, Parsnip Daily, to meet me at the palace in half an hour.'

Parsnip began to scribble furiously in the book. After

a few seconds that felt to Dwellings like a few hours, he
looked up and smiled.

'All done.'

'Very good. Right, I'm off to get some horses – I'll see
you at the palace, OK?'

Parsnip nodded at Dwellings, who turned and began
to walk away.

'Hey!' the tracker yelled after him. 'Come back here:
you forgot your book!'

Oblivious, Dwellings hurried outside, where his
patient assistant was waiting for him.

'Wheredad,' he snapped, grabbing the big man's arm.
'I need you to give me twenty minutes to find some
horses, then meet me at the palace. Bring Daily with
you; he'll never remember by himself.'

Wheredad said nothing, but he nodded and took a
seat at one of the outside tables. Parsnip Daily, indeed;
sometimes, he seriously doubted his employer's sanity.

Three

The palace was practically deserted when Dwellings arrived, dishevelled and miserable, in the front courtyard. He hadn't managed to find a single stable open and, worse still, he didn't like the look of the weather.

Wheredad raised a hand in greeting when he saw Dwellings approach.

Parsnip Daily was already crouched down beside the cart tracks, staring hard at the muddy imprint.

'How's he doing?' Dwellings whispered, creeping up to his assistant.

'All right,' Wheredad conceded. 'I bought him two pints at the Ferret and, funnily enough, it seemed to help clear up his memory problem. After that we went to the yard and studied the wheel-tread on the vegetable cart, then we came straight here.'

Time passed, and the duo waited patiently for the tracker to make an announcement of some sort.

A crow landed nearby, and Wheredad aimed a kick at it.

Time passed . . .

Parsnip pursed his lips and squinted at the ground, then looked up at the darkening sky and, finally, back to the cartwheel imprint.

'Well,' said Dwellings, exasperated by the prolonged silence. 'Do you recognise it?'

Parnsip nodded.

'Oh yeah, not a doubt in my mind . . . that's a cart track, all right.'

'Wonderful. Absolutely wonderful. Your skill simply takes my breath away. OF COURSE IT'S A BLOODY CART TRACK. I told YOU that, remember?'

'Yeah, but I'm saying that it's a cart, as opposed to a coach, see? The tracks are different.'

'I see. Well, that's very impressive, Mr Daily, but it doesn't help us much, does it?'

'Oh, right. So, what do you want to know, then?'

Dwellings prayed to the gods for strength.

'I want to know if you see the *same* tread that you saw on the wheels of the vegetable cart a while ago . . . and, if you do, I want you to track it,' he said, trying not to look at Wheredad's amused expression.

Parsnip stared at the tracks he'd been studying.

'That's 'em over there: third from the left.'

'And you can follow them?'

'No problem,' said Parsnip, merrily. 'You can track *anything*. Or, at least, *I* can. Mind you, it'll cost ya.'

'Money's no object.'

Parsnip nodded.

'Right you are, then. We'll call it a hundred and fifty crowns.'

'Done,' said Dwellings, before his assistant had time to argue.

The two men shook on the deal.

'Okey-dokey,' Parsnip said, clapping his hands with sudden enthusiasm. 'What're we trackin', a cart or a coach?'

'You can't be serious,' Wheredad muttered, eyeing the tracker with disbelief.

'Oh, I assure you, he is,' said Dwellings, dejectedly. He turned back to Parsnip. 'OK, Mr Daily, now listen up: I'm going to make things much simpler for you. I don't want you to talk, I don't want you to think, all I want, MISTER DAILY, is for you to follow those cart tracks, third from the end . . . or I will *kill* you. Do you understand that, MISTER DAILY?'

'Yeah.'

'How about now?'

'Still understand.'

'Very good. Then if I were you, I'd move myself . . .'

The tracker nodded and buttoned his coat, then put his head down and began to walk against the wind. Dwellings quickly followed after him, and motioned for Wheredad to do the same.

Surprisingly enough, Parsnip Daily didn't wander from his chosen path; it seemed that, contrary to all the evidence, when his mind was actually fixed on one specific idea, it didn't waver. Dwellings made a mental note of the fact in case it might prove useful in further dealings with the man.

Time passed . . .

He and Wheredad followed the tracker out of the palace gates, around Oval Square and along North Street. For one heart-stopping moment, Dwellings actually thought that Daily might have lost the cart's tracks at the top of North Street, but the tracker quickly pointed east and veered off along Royal Road. He eventually came to a grinding halt at the mouth of the Market Place.

'What is it?' said Dwellings, hurrying up to the tracker when he realised that Daily had stopped dead. 'Have you lost the trail?'

Parsnip shook his head.

'No,' he said simply.

'Well?' Dwellings exclaimed, deliberately ignoring the breathless puffs and pants of his lagging assistant. 'What's the problem?'

Parsnip shrugged noncommittally.

'Trail goes outside the city,' he said. 'I just wondered if you wanted to pick up those horses . . . and get my money.'

Dwellings and Wheredad shared a significant glance.

'Besides,' Parsnip continued, 'if we're going to track the thing, surely it's best to track it to its source?'

Dwellings' eyes lit up.

'You really think you can?'

'Oh, I reckon so. Might be a long trip, though; 'cause if I'm any judge, cartwheels with this tread were only knocked out near Crust way.'

'Didn't we think the lad on the veg cart was probably from Crust?' Wheredad hazarded.

Dwellings nodded, gravely.

'We did.' He turned back to the tracker. 'Daily; I need you to *continue* to follow those tracks – and listen, this is very important – try not to think of *anything* else while you're doing it.'

''Sfine,' said Daily, sniffing. 'I never *do*; tracking is my thing, remember?'

'Yes,' said Dwellings, trying not to think of how he'd had to remind the man that he was a tracker in the first place. 'Wheredad will stay with you. I'm going to get some reinforcements and meet you outside the city, assuming you've got that far by the time we catch you up. OK?'

'Reinforcements?' Wheredad grumbled. 'Do we really need any?'

Dwellings boggled at him. 'What if we find those responsible for kidnapping Lord Curfew? Do you seriously think you and I would be able to tackle whatever it was that took him, when an entire guard force couldn't get the job done? Ha!'

'So who're we going to get to come with us? A handful of those bonehead guards from the palace?'

Dwellings shook his head.

'No, of course not!' he said. 'We're looking for brave, heroic individuals who are willing to go to great risks for Lord and Country.'

'In Dullitch?' muttered Wheredad. 'Good luck.'

Dwellings said nothing else; he'd already thought of the perfect candidate, but there was absolutely no way on Illmoor that he was going to ask *him* . . .

Enoch Dwellings looked down at his feet, then up at the wall and, finally, straight at the vampire.

'So that's the story,' he said, trying to stop his wandering gaze straying towards the creature's annoying, curiously attractive daughter. 'I don't want *or* need you to join me on this endeavour but, as you said before, you do *owe* me a favour, so I've decided to call it in immediately.'

'Sounds fair to me,' said Lusa, quickly. 'Do we get a share in the glory?'

Dwellings and Obegarde both turned to regard her at the same time.

'What?'

'WHAT?'

'Well,' the girl continued. 'Do we both get to share in the praise if we actually find the viscount and return him unharmed?'

'Did I get a share in your father's glory when he was sneaking in here of a night, and stealing all my cases?'

Lusa shrugged off the accusation.

'That's different,' she said. '*This* could be dangerous. Under the circumstances, I think a small acknowledgement would be warranted if we all found the viscount together; agreed?'

Dwellings muttered something under his breath, then smiled rather falsely.

'I suppose so,' he snapped. 'What did you have in mind? A plain old chorus of halleluiahs or twenty-two golden geese singing about heroes and long-toothed warriors?'

Lusa smiled sweetly.

'No,' she said. 'Just a quick "the loftwing and his daughter helped" would be nice.'

'Yes,' Obegarde added. 'And maybe some talk of a *joint* practice?'

'WHAT?' Dwellings' eyes bulged in his head. 'You must be joking . . .'

'Why? We'd work well together; there's you with your incredible mind, me with my strength, my speed and *my daughter*, and Wheredad with . . . with . . . with whatever he's got.'

The words hung in the air for a few moments and then . . .

'We'll see,' said Dwellings, shaking Obegarde roughly by the hand and wincing when the vampire almost crippled him.

Obegarde beamed at him.

'Actually,' he said, 'I'm really glad you came back. It gives me a chance to show you this . . .'

He handed the ring to the detective.

'What is it?' said Dwellings, taking the ring and holding it up to the light.

'A ring with the royal seal on it; a hundred crowns says it's Curfew's.'

Dwellings nodded.

'Where did you find it?' he asked.

'The sewers,' said Obegarde, folding his arms over his chest. 'The shapeshifter dropped his spoils en route from the palace wine cellar; he must've come back for it.'

'But the palace is supposed to be on full alert!'

'With those morons guarding it? Don't make me laugh . . .'

Dwellings shook his head.

'But that doesn't make sense!' he snapped. 'Why would they kidnap Curfew and then come back for his ring . . . ?'

'Assuming it's the same lot, you mean?'

'Don't be stupid; of course it is! Hmm . . . maybe I should go and speak to Secretary Spires, find out what Curfew uses the ring for.'

'But I thought you said we needed to leave as soon as possible?'

'Yes,' Dwellings admitted. 'We do. I assume your daughter will be staying here?'

Lusa glared at him.

'You assume wrong, Mr Dwellings.'

'But it might be dangerous!'

'And?'

'And . . . and—'

'AND I'd like to bring someone else,' Obegarde interrupted, capitalising on Dwellings' momentary shock. 'Don't worry; he's very discreet.'

'Five crowns,' said Obegarde. He'd caught up with Jimmy Quickstint outside the Ferret and was trying, rather unsuccessfully, to recruit him for the tracking mission.

'Five crowns? To travel to Crust and back? Ha! Now I *know* you're joking.'

'Fifteen.'

'That's a bit of a jump, isn't it? Don't get excited, though: the answer's still "Forget It".'

'Twenty-five.'

'Don't you understand the word "no"?'

'Thirty.'

'I don't believe this,' said Jimmy, walking away from Obegarde with a half-smile on his face. 'I really don't. Why me?'

'Because I know I can trust you.'

Jimmy shook his head.

'Why can't I stay *here* and protect her?'

'Because she's determined to come with us!'

'Oh, for crying out loud.'

The gravedigger let out a heavy sigh, stopped walking and turned to face the vampire.

'You want me to follow you to donkey-knows-where just to watch out for your daughter?'

'Yes. Please.'

'But I'm no protection! You've said it yourself enough times; a strong breeze'd blow me over!'

Obegarde shrugged. 'Even so.'

'Look, I'm just not int—'

'OK, a hundred crowns . . . but you bring me a weapon as well.'

'Er . . . done.'

They shook hands, somewhat reluctantly on Jimmy's part.

'What sort of weapon are you after?' he enquired, squinting up at the vampire with an unrelenting smile on his face.

'Something small but devastating.'

'Right.'

'You can get hold of something like that?'

'Sure, it might cost you an extra twenty crowns or so, but I can get it, no problems.'

'Good. Can you meet me back here in, say, forty minutes?'

'Call it an hour . . . and I'll bring your lethal weapon with me.'

'Great.'

Jimmy nodded.

'So who are the other members of this search party?' he asked. 'And who or what are we lookin' for, as if I need to ask?'

The vampire smiled, weakly.

'You ever heard of Enoch Dwellings?'

'Only when you mentioned him in the sewers.'

'Well, *he's* leading the search with his assistant, Doctor Wheredad, and a tracker called Parsnip.'

'Parsnip?' Jimmy's eyes lit up. 'Parsnip Daily?'

'Yes, I think so.'

'Gods damn it; that bloke owes me twenty-five crowns!'

'Oh, right.' Obegarde grinned. 'We better not waste any time catching up with them, then.'

'I hear you,' said Jimmy, haring off down the street. 'Just wait in the Ferret! I'll be back in no time!'

Five

'Mr Enoch Dwellings, Master Secretary.'

The guard bowed low and departed, leaving a determined detective to stride openly to the scroll-cluttered desk that dominated the chamber.

'Mr Spires . . .'

'Good news, I hope,' said the royal secretary, without looking up.

'Well, it might be; yes.'

Spires looked up suddenly, eyebrows rising.

'Really?'

'Yes, we've located a tracker who has managed to identify the cart tracks outside; we think he should be able to follow the tracks to their source.'

'How extraordinary . . .' said Spires, somewhat aghast, 'And you've come to me because you require – what? Troops? Weaponry?'

'Neither, Master Secretary. What I *would* like to discover is the significance of this ring and its whereabouts in the palace when it was stolen . . .'

Spires immediately snatched the ring from the detective and, as he studied the item, his eyes bulged in his head and his mouth dropped open.

'Where – um – HOW did you get this? Do you have the other one?'

'There are two?'

'Yes! They were *both* accounted for after the viscount's disappearance, but they were *both* missing from his lordship's room this morning . . .'

Dwellings sighed.

'*This one* was dropped by a shapeshifter who was caught leaving the palace via the sewer system. Please don't ask me how I came by it: saves me having to lie to you.'

'A shapeshifter?' the secretary gasped. 'You mean half-man and half—'

'Snake, in this instance. Yes; a creature enchanted to morph from its original state into that of a human . . . and back again, as the need arises.'

Spires shuddered at the thought.

'Then the cursed wretch must've got away with the other one,' he said, turning the ring over and over in his fingers. 'To answer your question, this is a Seal Ring: a ring used to identify the viscount should anything . . . unspeakable . . . happen to him. It is also used in the coronation of a new Lord; it is *extremely* magical and would be of absolutely no use to a shapeshifter.'

Dwellings frowned.

'Oh? Why is that?'

'Because,' Spires went on, slumping in his chair, 'the Seal Ring is a ring enchanted to recognise bloodlines, and it can immediately identify its wearer. It would revert a shapeshifter back to its original form, and renders impostors naked in their treachery.'

'That's incredible! Who made it?'

'Lord Morban's sorcerer made them both, I believe; when the Tri-Age was still young. They're . . . priceless.'

'Yes,' said Dwellings, concerned. 'The kidnappers must have needed the rings very badly to come back for them.'

Spires nodded.

'Do hurry, Mr Dwellings,' he urged. 'I fear we haven't much time before the viscount is lost to us . . . for ever.'

'I hope you are wrong, Master Secretary. Good day to you . . .'

'Wait!'

Dwellings glanced over his shoulder.

'Sir?'

'Do you not require troops?'

'No, Master Secretary; I think it will only complicate

matters if we go in mob-handed . . . and it will be double the waste if our tracker fails to find the viscount's captors. Let us see what my small band can do on their own; then, if need be, I will come back to you for help.'

Spires nodded.

'You are a brave man, Enoch Dwellings. May the gods of Illmoor go with you!'

'Don't wish that on me, please! I need help, not hindrance . . .'

Spires watched the detective march out of his office, then rang the small hand-bell on the edge of his desk.

A stout butler hurried inside.

'Can I assist you, Master Secretary?'

'Yes, Brilling; I want nine guards and eleven horses in the outer courtyard in one hour.'

'Are the extra horses to be riderless, Master Secretary?'

Spires shook his head.

'No, Brilling: one's for me and the other is for the chairman of the city council. Now do move along, there's a good chap.'

'So WHO are they?' Curfew asked again, his voice suddenly edged with desperation.

Innesell took a moment to respond.

'Well, they're murderers,' he said. 'That's for sure; they killed everyone here: the innkeeper, the cook, *and* . . . um . . . the friend I was travelling with.'

Curfew noticed a distinct *lack* of sadness in the prisoner's voice as he finished.

'I'm sorry about your friend,' Curfew called, wondering if the two men had actually liked each other. 'Did you say they killed an innkeeper and a cook?'

'Yes; the two guys who ran the inn upstairs.'

'Upstairs? We're in a tavern?'

'We're underneath one.'

'Where is it, exactly?'

Innesell coughed a few times.

'On the road to Crust,' he said eventually. 'Don't you remember being brought down here? You struggled quite a bit, from what I heard . . .'

Curfew massaged his forehead, roughly.

'The last thing I remember was the assassin who came into my bedchamber,' he said, speaking into the hole. 'He had the drop on me, yet he seemed almost surprised when I fought back, which was odd . . .'

'Maybe he thought you were asleep?'

'Maybe. Anyway, I took up my sword, and rallied as best I could against the fiend, but he was . . .'

'Better? Stronger?'

'Hmm . . . faster, certainly. There was a lot of blood – his *and* mine – but I don't think he was the one who knocked me out in the end. There was an interruption, I recall, and others came into the room. Not guards; I think it was the cleaners I saw in the corridor outside. I thought they would help me, but they didn't: instead they all piled in, raining blows. It was a grim night: usually I'd have been prepared for an attack – I have to be on guard against such things, you see – but on this night there was a bad thunderstorm, and I was wearing earplugs. Ha! If only I'd heard them approaching, I could probably have taken them out.'

Innesell waited for the viscount to finish. Then he whispered:

'I'm guessing they were *all* wearing earplugs.'

'Oh? Why would you say that?'

'Because they took a Jenacle banshee with them.'

'A what?'

'A Jenacle banshee; a tiny, wailing ghoul. They've been breeding it for months. It was here, in the dungeon, before they kidnapped you.'

'Really? You saw it?'

'I *heard* it wail; that was enough. They say its death cry can put a man to sleep in half a second, and hearing it makes your ears bleed.'

Curfew drew in a breath.

'Hmm . . . So who's in charge here, d'you think?'

'I don't know,' said the voice of Innesell. 'I haven't actually met the leader . . .'

'D'you think there is one?'

'Oh, definitely. I've heard them talking about him; a pretty nasty character by all accounts.'

'I don't doubt it,' said Curfew, carefully. 'He could be the one I fought.'

Innesell's voice cut in quickly.

'No,' he said. 'The one you described sounds like the one they call Rhark; he's a master of blades and steel . . . claims to be the greatest swordsman in Illmoor, which undoubtedly he is.'

Curfew nodded to himself.

'Yes,' he agreed. 'That would certainly explain the skill. How many others are there?'

'Three that I know of,' said Innesell, his voice becoming shaky. 'Two shapeshifters and a man they call Kneath, who pretends to be the innkeeper.'

'Shapeshifters?' Curfew repeated. 'Really?'

'Yeah, I think one's a lion; the other is definitely a snake.'

Curfew started; a terrible thought had suddenly occurred to him.

'Innesell,' he called, softly. 'Why are you telling me all this?'

His answer was an incredible eruption of mocking laughter, which rang out through the dungeon and echoed all around the room.

'Innesell indeed,' the voice cackled. 'Exactly how gullible *are* you?'

Despite the shock, Viscount Curfew fought to remain calm.

'Gullible enough, it would seem,' he muttered.

'But no fool,' added the voice. 'And certainly no slouch with a sword – you're the first man to give me a cut in more than fifteen years! Still, I'm sure that it's my master that you are dying to meet. Fret not, Lord Curfew, for that time has come . . .'

There was a moment of silence, followed by an approach of footsteps from the corridor outside.

A torch struck up, the door was unlatched and a

number of shadowy figures lurched into the cell. At length they parted to reveal a tall, hooded stranger, who strode towards the viscount with a terrible sense of purpose, cracking his jaw as he walked.

Curfew pulled himself on to his feet.

'Who ARE you?' he demanded.

'If you'll permit me, *my lord*,' said a familiar voice, 'I'll show you.'

The hood was drawn back and Curfew stared at the face behind it, a face he was not expecting to see but nevertheless recognised immediately.

After all, he saw it every morning . . . in the mirror.

Seven

When Enoch Dwellings arrived at the city gates, leading
a solid-looking horse behind his own princely mount,
Wheredad was standing alone.

'Where's Daily?' the detective enquired.

'He's gone on ahead,' said Wheredad, rolling his eyes.
'Said to catch him up. Did you manage to find us some
help, Enoch?'

'Yes,' Dwellings replied, avoiding the man's eyes. 'I've
asked the vampire to come along; just this once, you
understand.'

'Yes, Enoch: I think I understand. Is his daughter
coming?'

'That's got absolutely nothing to do with it!'

'I never said it had!'

'You implied it!'

'I didn't, Enoch! It's all in your own head.'

Dwellings felt his teeth begin to grit, and tried to calm himself by thinking happy thoughts; unfortunately, these all involved the vampire's daughter, so he quickly knocked *that* idea on the head.

'Just listen to yourself, will you?' he snapped instead. 'We need to keep our minds on the task ahead.'

'My mind IS on the task ahead,' Wheredad protested. 'It's *your* mind I'm concerned abo—'

'Shut up! I don't want to hear another word about it.'

He made a face and pointed to the second horse, which Wheredad then made several half-hearted attempts to mount. Eventually, the lumbering assistant managed the feat, and together the two men urged their steeds into a reluctant trot.

'Aren't we going to wait for Obegarde?' Wheredad hazarded.

Dwellings shook his head.

'We follow Daily; Obegarde follows us: it's quite simple, my friend. Now let's move, shall we? He can't be more than a few minutes ahead of us . . .'

The detective dug in his heels and his horse rocketed out of the palace gates. Wheredad attempted to follow suit, and almost lost his head in the process.

* * *

'This,' said Obegarde, staring blankly at the small creature that Jimmy had deposited squarely on his palm, 'is a hamster.'

The atmosphere in the Rotting Ferret had put the vampire in a bleak mood, but it could no way prepare him for the sight of Jimmy's promised weapon.

'Hey, that's not just *any* hamster,' the gravedigger protested. 'That's Kyn Blistering's own special, personal, favourite hamster from his legendary collection of death-dealers.'

'Yes, but it's *a hamster*, Jimmy.'

'And?'

'AND? AND! I asked for a ballistic weapon of major proportions, and you give me some eight-year-old's pet rodent.'

'You don't understand—'

'No, *you* don't understand: I need a heavy-duty crossbow, not a bloody straw-eater.'

'But, listen, it's KYN BLISTERI—'

'I don't care whose damn hamster it is! I don't care if it's the personal, magical pet of Hop Along Flong, the hamster-wielding lord of the lizardmen, it's still a wriggly little furball AND NOT a sawn-off scimitar.'

Jimmy waited patiently for the vampire to finish his rant, then smiled, in spite of the glare coming from the other end of the table.

'I dare you to annoy it,' he said.

'You what?'

'I DARE you . . .'

'To annoy the hamster?'

'Yeah.'

'Oh, you can't be serious . . .'

'Go on, then.'

'HOW in the name of sanity am I supposed to annoy a hamster?'

Jimmy shrugged.

'Flick its ear or something; make fun of it.'

'If you think for one second I'm talking to a hamster in the middle of the Ferret, you're sorely mistaken.'

'All right then, pull its leg or something . . .'

'You're INSANE, Jimmy.'

'Ha! You're frightened to upset it, aren't you?'

'I'm not even going to dignify *that* with an answer.'

'Oh well, *I'll* have to show you then . . .'

Jimmy crouched down and placed the hamster on the straw-strewn floor of the inn. Then he raised his leg and prepared to bring his boot down hard on the shaking rodent.

'What are you doing?' Obegarde demanded. 'You'll crush the thing!'

Jimmy grinned.

'You'd think so, wouldn't you?'

He brought his foot down, hard, to the accompaniment of a very brief squeak.

Jimmy looked down, a terrible expression on his face.

'You're right,' Obegarde observed, stroking his chin. 'It looks really mad.'

Jimmy lifted a leg, looked at the bottom of his shoe.

'I don't understand it,' he said, his lower lip trembling. 'That hamster was supposed to be *invincible*.'

'I'm not sure about that,' said Obegarde, whistling between his teeth. 'But I wouldn't be surprised if it came back to haunt you.'

He stood, walked over to the bar and deposited his empty tankard on the counter.

'Who is Kyn Blistering, anyway?'

'You really don't know?'

'I wouldn't ask if I *knew*, would I?'

Jimmy sighed. 'Well, Kyn Blistering was this incredible wizard: he used to magically enhance small creatures so that they grew in size when they were annoyed. He used to have rats ten metres long, spiders three metres tall, and there was even talk of a flea the size of a monkey. And they were all INVULNERABLE.'

'And who told you about Kyn Blistering?'

Jimmy shrugged.

'This guy I met in the Market Place on Wednesday lunchtime.'

'Right.' Obergarde nodded. 'Did he, by any chance, sell you the hamster as well?'

'Yeah! How did you know that?'

The vampire shrugged.

'Just psychic, I guess.' He clambered to his feet. 'Oh well, so much for weapons of mass destruction,' he muttered, heading towards the door of the inn. 'I'll have to settle for you, won't I?'

Jimmy glanced fearfully at the squashed hamster, then picked it up, put it in his breast pocket and mooched guiltily after Obegarde. His mood was not improved when they arrived outside, where a handsome young woman was waiting with two sturdy-looking horses. Jimmy felt uncomfortable almost immediately, and began to sweat.

'Your daughter?' he guessed, nodding politely at the girl, who smiled back.

'Indeed it is,' said Obegarde, patting the gravedigger companionably on the shoulder and whispering into his ear: 'Don't even think about it.'

Eight

Afternoon found Parsnip Daily fast approaching an old boarding house that sat like a fat and lonely pigeon on the road out of Dullitch. He didn't know this, of course; his attention was entirely focused on the road ahead of him. In fact, his concentration on the cart tracks was such that he walked straight into the front door of the property, causing the owner to come bolting out of the kitchen as if she were under attack by the hordes of hell. Daily observed, as he cowered back in surprise, that the woman was also armed with a heavy-duty shovel.

'What the bloody hell do you think you're doing?' she spat, showering him in the process. 'You're trespassin' on private property. Now get out of here or I'll do for you with me spade, right and proper.'

'You would as well, wouldn't you?' Daily gasped, rolling over and struggling to his feet. 'As a matter of fact, fine lady, I'm here to . . . to . . . er . . . to . . .'

'You're here to what? Break in? Steal my washing-up water?'

'NO! I was . . . er . . .'

'Scoutin' the place out for a raid later tonight, ya scum-suckin' little maggot—'

'NO! I've got this memory problem, you see . . .'

'You'll have more than a memory problem when I'm finished with you . . .'

Daily shook his head, as if trying to dislodge a thought. 'I'm sure I was . . .'

'Well?'

'Um . . .'

'On official business,' finished Enoch Dwellings, riding up behind the tracker and glaring down at the landlady with all the self-importance he could muster. 'I can certainly vouch for that.'

The woman grimaced up at him.

'And who the 'ell are you?' she demanded.

'I,' came the reply, 'am Enoch Dwellings, master detective . . . and the small dot you can see on the horizon is my assistant: not much of a horserider, I'm afraid.'

The landlady sniffed.

'What's your business 'ere?'

Dwellings leaned down and had a brief, but rather hushed, conversation with the tracker. Then he righted himself again.

'Is this your boarding house?' he asked, nodding at the large building with the 'Mrs Meaker's Boarding House' plaque hanging over the front porch.

The landlady nodded.

'Yeah; what of it?'

'We have reason to believe that you are housing criminals of the worst order,' Dwellings went on, dismounting with incredible aplomb.

'Rubbish,' snapped Mrs Meaker. 'We're empty.'

'Empty?' Dwellings echoed, raising an eyebrow. 'Are you sure?'

Mrs Meaker sniffed, and gobbed a globule of phlegm on to the floor.

' 'Bout as sure as a woman can be,' she said.

'I see,' said Dwellings, giving Daily a significant glance. 'Have you been vacant for long?'

Mrs Meaker shook her head.

'Oh no, we had a full house here earlier in the week.'

Dwellings' face lit up like a lantern.

'How many?' he asked.

'Er . . . three of 'em, there were.'

'Did they all arrive at the same time?'

'Yeah.'

'On a cart?'

'Yep.'

'A cart covered in dustsheets?'

'Dunno. I didn't bother to look.'

Wheredad arrived at the house, holding on to his horse as if he'd just been on a journey to purgatory and back.

'Do you remember what they looked like?' Dwellings continued, trying to stop his hands shaking.

'Yeah,' said Mrs Meaker, rubbing her hands together. 'Though my own memory's not been that great lately . . .'

Dwellings smiled at her knowingly and, reaching into his pocket, produced a handful of crowns.

'Will this help?' he said, extending his hand.

Mrs Meaker counted the coins.

'I doubt it,' she said, miserably.

'How about this,' said Wheredad, passing over a money pouch of his own.

'Ah,' said Mrs Meaker, scratching her ear. 'I feel something coming back . . .'

'It's a miracle,' muttered Dwellings, darkly.

'If my mind serves me well,' she chattered, greedily pocketing both offerings while she spoke, 'there was a big, bruisy sort, a thin, shifty little bloke and a young man with scars and a 'ead o' blond 'air. Don't quote me on it, mind . . .'

'Oh, we won't,' said Dwellings, biting his lip to stop himself exploding with anger. 'You don't know which direction they came from, do you?'

Mrs Meaker licked her lips, then pointed north.

'You know,' she said, 'I reckon they was from around . . .'

'. . . Crust way?'

'Yeah! Their clothes were kinda funny, you know. All except the blond one; he wore a sort o' cloak with a funny 'ood on it.'

Dwellings nodded, and remounted his horse.

'We're leaving,' he said. 'Daily, see if you can find the track further up the road.'

'Aren't we going to search the house?' Wheredad enquired, grabbing at the reins of his own beast.

'Well,' said the detective, dismissively, 'I very much doubt if they've hidden you-know-who in a boarding house on the main Dullitch Road, but you're more than welcome to look if you've a mind to . . .'

'Oi!' called Mrs Meaker, suddenly feeling left out of the conversation. 'What's all this about, exac'ly?'

'I don't know,' Dwellings shouted back, forcing his horse into a steady trot. 'How much is it worth to tell you?'

Nine

Obegarde, Lusa and Jimmy Quickstint galloped out of
Dullitch on two old but nevertheless remarkably fast
horses.

The vampire reached back and slapped the flank of
his steed, causing it to bolt on ahead for a time, but he
was soon caught up.

'Couldn't we have found another ride?' yelled Jimmy,
trying not to wince when the vampire's daughter
breathed in his ear. He hadn't been this close to a woman
since he'd sat on his grandmother's knee.

'Don't worry,' Lusa said, ducking a tree branch that
Jimmy gave her no warning of. 'I'm sure we can manage
just fine; would you, er, would you like me to lead?'

'No,' said Jimmy, quickly, wondering what he'd need to hold on to if their positions were reversed. 'I get sick if I'm on the back.'

They rode on down the Dullitch road, past acres of thick forest, lines of burnt-out mills and an old and somewhat dilapidated guest house, where a large, aggressive-looking woman stood in the garden, shaking her fist at two shrinking shapes in the distance.

'That's them,' said Obegarde, pointing in the same direction.

'How can you tell?' said Jimmy, trying not to breath out in case his stomach flopped over his trousers.

'It's easy,' said Obegarde, pointing back at the landlady. 'Dwellings is the only person I know who gets people that mad . . .'

Ten

'You're me?' said Curfew, peering at his captor.

'No,' said the impostor, 'but the resemblance is remarkable, isn't it?'

'Sorcery,' Curfew snapped, wishing he had a sword. 'Either that or you're a shapeshifter.'

'You were closer with your first guess, Viscount, though I do have two very talented shapeshifters in my service; it took me a long time to find them.'

'Who *are* you?'

'That is not important. What is important is that we are determined to take the throne of Illmoor for ourselves, and we will not be kept from the task by any . . . minor inconveniences.'

Curfew took a step back into the shadows, and his face darkened.

'What makes you think you have any right to my kingdom?' he asked.

'Nothing at all, Lord Curfew,' said the impostor. 'But then . . . we do intend to take it, all the same. Davenpaw! Rhark! Please show this noble wretch the meaning of the word "pain" . . .'

Footsteps approached, and the cell door swung open. Before Curfew had a chance to leap at his captor, a heavy-set man with a thick shock of hair entered the room and began to crack his knuckles. Curfew recognised him as one of the deliverymen he had interrupted in the palace corridor on the night of his kidnapping. The man was followed, at length, by the swordfighter Curfew had fallen to the same evening.

The viscount snarled.

'If it isn't Innesell,' he said, mockingly.

Rhark smiled at the mention of the name.

'I know, I know: pure genius, wasn't it?'

'Stay back,' Curfew warned, pulling himself along the wall as his attackers advanced. 'If you attempt to harm me in any way . . .'

'. . . you'll what?' Davenpaw asked, to mocking laughter from his companion. 'Banish us from your kingdom? Hahahaha!' He continued to crack his knuckles.

Curfew took a deep breath.

'Listen, I have power . . .'

'We know that,' said the voice of the impostor, from the doorway, 'and very soon it will be *our* power.'

Curfew finally managed to pull himself away from the wall. He held his hands in front of him.

'B-but you've made a terrible mistake . . .'

'Oh really?'

The impostor clapped his hands and the two servants parted to afford him a better view of the viscount.

'And what might that be, exactly?'

Curfew took a deep breath, and tried to keep his voice level as he spoke.

'I'll tell you if you let me live,' he mumbled, annoyed at himself for the fear that was eating away at him.

The royal impostor smiled, and tapped his lips with a thin finger.

'Hmm . . . an interesting proposition.'

The two aggressors backed away a little more, as their master deliberated.

'OK,' he said, eventually. 'You tell me what it is that I'm supposed to have missed and I'll let you live on down here indefinitely.'

Curfew staggered back, licking his cracked lips.

'I have your word?' he prompted.

The impostor nodded, and entered the cell.

'You do.'

'Very well. You may have me, but you don't have one

of my Seal Rings; you'll find that you need one in order to be crowned Lord of Dullitch.'

The impostor smiled, a dark and insipid grin that conspired to make him look even more menacing than he had done in the corridor outside.

'Thank you for telling me my mistake,' he said, sarcastically. 'But please don't worry unduly on my behalf: I do, in fact, have one of the rings of which you speak. My slithering friend kindly retrieved it from the depths of that pathetically guarded hovel you call a palace. We would have got them both if it wasn't for an unfortunate incident in the sewers: still, I'm not greedy.'

He reached into his pocket and produced one of the viscount's unmistakable Seal Rings.

Curfew grimaced.

'If my home is such a disgrace, impostor, then why do you go to such lengths to steal it?'

The shade-viscount burst into fits of laughter.

'Haha! But when *I* rule the capital, my palace will be like no other in the history of Illmoor! The city shall shine with the splendour of a thousand marble towers, the harbour will be awash with trading ships and I shall rebuild the great Elistalis in my own secret image, for ever mocking the curtain drawn over the eyes of your dim-witted citizens! Hahahahaha! Oh, and I'm afraid I'm going to kill you anyway . . .'

The impostor slipped the Seal Ring on to his finger and grinned.

'I wish you luck in your endeavour,' Curfew spat, a sudden surge of confidence enabling him to mock the awed tones of his enemy. 'But I assure you that you won't need to build the Elistalis in your secret image . . .'

The impostor's smile didn't fade, but his nostrils flared. 'And what is that supposed to mean?'

'It means that the Seal Ring is itself enchanted . . . and when you put it on, your true identity will be revealed.' Curfew beamed a smile of his own, then hawked up some phlegm and spat on the floor at his captor's feet. 'It's a defensive mechanism, so that the throne can never be taken by anyone not of the blood. It takes a few seconds, so you'll start to feel the effects right about now. The best thing is: there's absolutely nothing you can do about it . . .'

A slap from the man called Davenpaw almost knocked the viscount senseless; Curfew flew back against the wall, collapsing to the ground and badly jarring his shoulder. From his prone position, he stared up in frank disbelief at the impostor, who had remained icily calm and whose features were unaltered.

'I don't understand,' Curfew cried, his voice now fraught with despair. 'You're not changing!'

The impostor leaned over the viscount.

'No, *my lord*, I am not . . . and you might venture to ask yourself why . . . ?'

Curfew shook his head, as if trying to dislodge the terrible thought he was having.

'Y-you can't be of the blood!' he screamed. 'You can't be!'

The impostor shrugged.

'Can I not? Oh ... then how am I able to defy the enchanted ring? Some extra special sorcery, perhaps? I can weave dreams and change skins, *my lord*, but I can assure you that my powers do not extend to countering the effects of ancient magic!' He turned to his hesitant servants. 'Rhark; I want you to sharpen my sword: I think I'll dispatch the good viscount myself.'

'B-but you said I could finish him, master! You promised!'

'Silence, man! Just do as you're told, or else you can join him!'

Rhark stuttered and gabbled an answer, then bowed and departed.

'Very good,' snapped the impostor, turning to Davenpaw. 'And you, my friend, can stay here to teach this noble fool a lesson he will never forget, at least for the remainder of his all too few hours.' With that, he turned and swept out of the room.

Viscount Curfew grimaced as silence descended on the cell, and the hairy giant came lumbering towards him ...

Eleven

'I don't like to brag,' Daily said, as Dwellings rode up beside him, 'but this is going to be a walk in the park for me.'

'Oh?' said the detective, somewhat doubtfully. 'And why is that, exactly?'

'The tracks,' Daily replied, squinting up at his new employer with a gap-toothed grin. 'They're the easiest tracks I've ever followed; the imprint is really distinctive, and the pacing of the cart makes the whole run impossible to lose sight of.'

Dwellings pursed his lips.

'I'm glad you're so confident,' he said. 'So how long do you think it's going to take us to track these folks down? A day? Two?'

Daily put his head on one side, looked up at Dwellings with a thoughtful expression.

'Let me see if I can make out the tracks from where you are,' he said, climbing up behind the detective.

'You won't be able to,' Dwellings muttered, offering the tracker a helping hand. 'It all just looks like uneven ground from up he—'

'I can see 'em fine,' Daily announced, as Wheredad trotted up beside them. Obegarde and the others were following him at a distance.

'You can?' Dwellings gasped, staring at the tracker in frank astonishment.

'No sweat,' said Daily, with a wink. 'If we can get on the gallop, I reckon we'll be a good way along before dark: really all depends where these boys have dumped their cart. I mean, they'd have to be really stupid to keep it, wouldn't they?'

The detective nodded.

'However, I regularly find that criminals are devilishly clever with the intricate stuff and angelically stupid when it comes to the obvious.' He smiled at the thought. 'Can we get going?'

'Yeah,' said Daily. 'Let's just wait a few minutes for the others to catch up, then we'll hare off at a whip. We only need to stop every few miles, so I can squint at the tracks a bit, see where they're headed.'

'Sounds good to me, Enoch,' Wheredad admitted, suppressing a deep yawn.

Dwellings beamed.

'You're a wonder, Daily,' he said, with a grin. 'You're a regular wonder.'

Meanwhile . . .

The scout brought his horse to a stop on the crest of the hill, produced an elegant spyglass and studied the view very carefully.

'I see them, Master Secretary,' he called back. 'They're just off the main-road; looks like they're heading into woodland.'

'Very good,' Spires shouted. 'Now come back down from there; we don't want to make our position too obvious.' He turned to Burnie, the troglodyte councillor whose horse was riding level with his own. 'What should we give them, d'you think? Half an hour's lead? An hour? Any more than that, it'll start to get dark and we'll end up losing them.'

'Agreed,' Burnie sniffled, picking some mucus from his slimy head and attaching it, for reasons best known to himself, to the base of an ear. 'It always pays to be cautious, but I think we should stay as close as possible.'

Spires nodded.

'Half an hour it is, then,' he said, turning his attention to the mounted guards. 'I don't suppose anyone thought to bring a pack of cards?'

Twelve

Viscount Curfew awoke, battered and bruised, his ribs sore from Davenpaw's beating and eyes swollen where the big man had rammed his head against the brickwork.

He tried to raise himself up on his cracked hands, but even when he found his feet, he discovered that he lacked the will to stand . . .

Better to sleep, he reflected, better to store up as much strength as possible in preparation for the battle ahead.

For most undoubtedly, there would be one . . .

Part Four

Lostings

One

There was still an hour of daylight left in the sky when the horse carrying Enoch Dwellings and the tracker, Parsnip Daily, trotted out from the edge of a small wood and emerged on a rise overlooking a wide patchwork of fields.

'It's very beautiful, up this way,' the detective observed, as Daily leaped down from the mount, snatched a stubby spyglass from his jerkin and scrutinised the landscape. 'Don't you think so, Parsnip?'

'Yeah: I don't reckon your assistant is too impressed, though . . .'

Dwellings glanced back at Wheredad, who was fast asleep in the saddle. His horse looked unaccountably moody.

'He must be tired,' Dwellings observed, rather unnecessarily.

'You think?'

'Mmm . . . are the tracks getting more difficult to follow?'

'No.'

'Good: do you think we're getting close?'

The tracker didn't reply, but maintained his study of the land, switching his attention from the tracks on the ground to the spyglass, and back again.

Sensing his companion's preoccupation, Dwellings turned his horse around and trotted up to Obegarde and Jimmy, who were discussing a famous sword-fight they'd seen re-enacted in the town square a few weeks before. Lusa, Enoch noticed, looked bored to tears.

He brushed back a lock of his hair, urged his horse to trot beside Jimmy's, leaned over to the girl and said: 'Excuse me . . .'

Lusa turned and smiled at him.

'Hiya.'

'Afternoon, Are you enjoying your—'

'Oi! You lot!'

The entire party, including a very resentful Enoch Dwellings, whipped around to face the tracker, who was still staring through his spyglass.

'We've got a solitary building at two o'clock.'

'Eh?' Jimmy shouted. 'It's five-past six!'

'No, he means two o'clock *directionally*,' Lusa

translated. 'You know, two o'clock-clock.' She pointed with her arm to indicate the view-path.

'But it's five-past six,' said Jimmy again, about as quick on the uptake as he was getting out of bed in the morning.

'Hmm . . . can you see what sort of building it is?' Dwellings asked, as he and Obegarde trotted up to where Daily was standing.

'Yeah,' the vampire added. 'Are we talking a cottage or a castle, here?'

'It's more like an inn, actu'lly,' said Parsnip, folding the spyglass away. 'And the tracks are definitely heading that way. Why don't we find a spot to tether up the horses? If we're on foot, we can keep to the edge of the woods and get a better view without being seen.'

'You've lost them?' Spires exclaimed, sharing a look of disbelief with the troglodyte chairman. 'What do you mean, you've lost them?'

'Don't panic, Mr Secretary,' said Burnie, dismissing the embarrassed guard before he could splutter an audible reply. 'It's easily done, especially in a wood like this. If we look around long enough, we'll find them.'

'B-but this is ridiculous! This wood isn't even particularly big!'

Burnie rolled his eyes.

'Exactly, Mr Secretary. So we'll find them in plenty of time, won't we?'

'Really!' Spires snapped back. 'Is that plenty of time to save the viscount, or plenty of time to save the morons we're following?'

The little troglodyte put his head down and ordered his horse to the head of the group.

'We'll try this way first!' he shouted back to the Guard Sergeant. 'It looks like the most . . . disturbed path.'

Two

The inn stood alone in a rough patch of land where no flowers grew. All the trees surrounding the building bowed away from it, as if they didn't want to get too close for fear of doom.

An ageing sign swung back and forth on creaky hinges, announcing: 'Welcome to Lostings: drink up and go'.

'Drink up and go,' said Jimmy, peering through Obegarde's spyglass and reading the sign aloud. 'Nice words; they can't value custom much, can they?'

Dwellings massaged his brow.

'Do you think Curfew's captors stayed here?' he asked the tracker, hopefully.

Daily put his head on one side, and grimaced.

'The tracks definitely lead up there,' he said. 'We should take a look.'

'I agree,' said Dwellings, reaching out an arm to hold the others back. '*You* should take a look.'

'Why me?' said Daily, resentfully.

'Because you're the tracker . . . and no one else will be able to identify the right imprints!'

'Well, can I take someone with me?'

'No, you'll make better time on your own.'

'But what if I get attacked?'

Dwellings sighed.

'If you get attacked, which is highly unlikely in my opinion, we will see it through the spyglass and we'll be there in an instant. OK?'

'Hmm . . . if you say so.'

'I do.'

Daily muttered something under his breath, then turned and idled off in the direction of Lostings Inn. He was back in just under three minutes.

'What was I looking for again?'

'The cart tracks, you moron!'

'Hey, don't speak to him like that,' Lusa interjected. 'He's human, you know; he has *feelings*.'

'*You* don't understand,' Dwellings warned, waggling a finger under the girl's nose. 'If I don't speak to him like that, he'll forget everything I say to him! He has a memory problem, you see . . .'

'Right,' Lusa said, nodding. 'So if he has a memory problem then it's not going to matter *how* you speak to him, he's still going to forget it. So shall we try a little compassion?' She turned to Daily with the sweetest smile from her Kindness Arsenal. 'Mr Daily,' she crooned, 'do you think that you could sneak over to the inn and tell us if the cart tracks from Dullitch Palace continue past it?'

'Right.'

'And also,' she continued, 'could you pop into the inn and ask them if they've had any customers who arrived in a cart from the south?'

Daily nodded eagerly.

'No problem,' he said, haring off towards Lostings with renewed vigour.

'Very nicely put,' said Dwellings, sarcastically. 'A crown says he's back in less than five minutes.'

Lusa shrugged.

'Make it two, and you're on.'

'Deal.'

The five companions stood quietly in the shade of the trees as Daily became a small figure in the middle distance and, eventually, disappeared around the back of the inn.

'Time passed . . .'

'Two crowns, please,' said Lusa, winking devilishly.

Dwellings clenched his fists.

'The idiot's not back yet,' he snapped.

'But he's been gone six minutes.'

'No he hasn't; it's more like four.'

'Actually, he *has* been gone five minutes,' Wheredad chirped. 'I counted.'

'You COUNTED?' Dwellings exclaimed, his respect for the man at an all-time low.

'Sorry, Enoch: I was bored.'

The detective glared at him.

'Find the cart tracks from the palace,' Daily muttered to himself, walking around the inn with his head down and his eyes locked on the ground.

'The cart tracks from the palace,' he repeated. 'The cart from the palace tracks: can't forget that I need to find the palace cart. Hang on a minute – the palace cart? That doesn't sound right – they'd have a coach at the palace, surely . . . maybe it's a coach I'm looking for . . . but what about the tracks? I was looking for tracks, wasn't I?'

Daily came to a sudden standstill. Within ten seconds, he couldn't remember whether he'd just come out of the inn or was making his way inside . . .

Then he remembered a face – quite a pretty one – and a vampire who was not so pretty, but nevertheless striking . . .

. . . and, suddenly, Parsnip Daily knew exactly what he was looking for.

Three

'Well?' said Dwellings, when Daily eventually made his
way back to the party. 'Did you ask them if they'd seen
the vegetable cart?'

The tracker shook his head.

'No,' he said, flatly.

'I knew it!' Wheredad exclaimed. 'I told you it was
pointless getting *him* to go in – he probably forgot three
seconds after you told—'

'Actually, I didn't forget what you said,' Daily chirped.
'I had other reasons for not asking them.'

'You had other reasons?' Obegarde ventured, folding
his arms in a disgruntled fashion. 'Like what?'

Daily shrugged.

'Well,' he said. 'I *hate* talking to people I don't know, and I especially hate visiting taverns without buying a drink.'

'Is that it?' Wheredad said, aghast. '*Those* are your reasons for not asking them about the cart?'

'Yeah,' said Daily, yawning. 'Well, that and the fact that the tracks stop round the back.'

There was a moment of shocked silence.

'What did you say?' said Dwellings, checking to make sure his ears weren't blocked.

Obegarde, Wheredad and Lusa shared a glance. Even Jimmy smiled.

'The tracks stop?' Dwellings prompted.'You mean we've found the place where the cart ended its journey?'

'Yep,' said Daily, snapping his fingers and winking proudly. 'And in record time, too, 'case you're interested. I reckon—'

'Is there another cart there, by any chance?' the detective cut in.

'Yeah,' said Daily. 'It's full o' white sheets.'

'Hey,' Jimmy began, a clueless expression on his face. 'If the tracks end there, do you think the owners are inside? You know, having a drink or something?'

'I doubt it,' said Daily, sniffing. 'When I looked through the window of the place, there was only the barman in there.'

'OK,' Dwellings commented, scratching the bridge of

his nose with a coin. 'I think we should go in as drinkers first, look the place over.'

'What, all of us?' said Obegarde, a smirk brewing on his face. 'Won't that look a bit obvious?'

Dwellings shook his head.

'Not all of us,' he said. 'We'll go in separately.'

'You really think that'll make a difference?' muttered Lusa, pushing her way to the front of the group. 'Let's reason it out, shall we? A tavern in the middle of nowhere that has, at present, no punters, is about to get five *really* unusual customers in the space of a few minutes?'

Dwellings shrugged.

'When you put it like that, it *does* seem a little peculiar . . .'

'Exactly,' finished the girl, getting into her stride as the group thinker. 'I say that one of us should go in through the front door as a distraction, while somebody else creeps in through the back, assuming there's a back door? Is there a back door, Parsnip?'

'There's a cellar hatch,' Daily confirmed.

'Right, a cellar hatch. Good. The rest of us should probably stay here and see what happens.'

'Sounds like a good plan,' Dwellings agreed, 'that, with one minor adjustment, could become a brilliant plan.'

Lusa's smile floated on her face.

'What minor adjustment?' she asked, sweetly.

'Well, Wheredad and myself will go into the bar, posing as ramblers, while Obegarde and Jimmy sneak in through the cellar hatch . . .'

'. . . leaving Daily and myself out here on our own?' Lusa turned to Parsnip with a smile. 'Should've seen that one coming, shouldn't we?'

'It's for the best, I think,' Obegarde added. 'It could be very dangerous in there . . .'

'Yeah,' agreed Daily. 'And I'm a tracker, not a mercenary . . . from what I can remember.'

The door of the inn swung open, and Dwellings strode inside. He was followed, a few seconds later, by a puffing, panting Wheredad.

'Good evening,' he exclaimed, peering around the room and noting a) the crackling fire, b) the incredible lack of clean straw on the floors and c) the brooding innkeeper who looked as if he'd been propped up behind the bar.

'Can I 'elp you?' said the last, placing both hands flat on the bar top in a manner which managed to be both enquiring *and* warlike at the same time.

'Two ales, please, bartend,' said Dwellings, sweeping confidently to the bar and flinging his coat on to a nearby stand. 'One for myself and one for my rambling companion.'

The innkeeper cast Wheredad a measuring glance, then nodded at Dwellings and made himself busy behind the bar.

'We're not from around here,' said the detective, raising his voice a tone higher for reasons best known to himself.

'I'd never have guessed,' said the innkeeper, belching as he laid two heavy tankards on the bar top. 'That all?'

'Yes,' said Dwellings, smiling. 'Unless you do dinners here?'

The innkeeper nodded sullenly.

'We do.'

'Oh . . .'

'I'll go out the back and get you a menu—'

'NO!'

The big man paused en route to an inner door, and turned around slowly.

'No?'

Dwellings made an effort to disguise the urgency in his voice.

'I mean, don't bother,' he said, with a mock laugh. 'I'm not really that hungry and I don't suppose for one second that my friend is peckish either.'

'Well, actually—'

'Quiet, MAN!'

The innkeeper looked from the detective to his assistant and back again.

'You two just escaped from somewhere?' he ventured.

'Ha!' said Dwellings, spilling some of his pint as he raised the tankard shakily to his lips. 'Did you hear that, old friend? Escaped from somewhere indeed! Hahahahaha!'

Wheredad added some mock laughter of his own, but the sound soon died away when the innkeeper began to scrub the bar top with a dark, filthy-looking cloth.

Jimmy Quickstint peered round the back wall of the inn, checked that the coast was clear, and made a signal with his thumb and forefinger.

A heartbeat later, Jimmy and Obegarde tiptoed along the length of the wall, sneaked behind the cart (still laden with dustsheets), and crouched down beside the inn's sizeable cellar hatch.

'That's one hell of a big padlock,' Obegarde observed, reaching down carefully and weighing the lock in his clawed hand.

'It's nothing,' Jimmy assured him. 'Trust me; I've broken bigger padlocks than that in my sleep.'

'Really?' said Obegarde, impressed by the brag. 'C'mon, then; let's see you prove it.'

Jimmy snaked a hand into his trouser pocket and pulled out a small bunch of thin metal clips.

Then he proceeded to work each one into the lock until there was an audible 'click' and the padlock came open.

'Wow,' muttered Obegarde. 'I can't believe you actually did that.'

Jimmy nodded.

'As I said, in my sleep.' He peered into the cellar beyond. 'Dark down there, isn't it?'

'Yep,' said Obegarde.

'Don't suppose you thought to bring a lantern or anything?'

'Nope. Sometimes I can see in the dark; but it depends whether my eyes are playing up . . .'

'Terrific,' Jimmy muttered. 'Comforting to know that I'm working with the best . . .'

He inched a foot down on to the top of what looked to be a dangerously fractured staircase and slowly began to descend. Obegarde followed, thinking twice about shutting the hatch behind him.

At length, they emerged into a large and extremely spacious cellar lit with wall-torches. The room was featureless apart from two empty barrels, a stout door and a floor-to-ceiling tapestry depicting some ancient battle between the mage lords of Illmoor.

Jimmy turned to Obegarde in the half dark, and grinned.

'Are you thinking what I'm thinking?' he whispered.

'Depends,' whispered Obegarde, still looking around

him. 'Are you thinking that they don't stock up much on ale?'

Jimmy shook his head, nodding towards the near wall. 'I'm thinking that there's a tunnel behind that tapestry.'

Obegarde mooched over to it.

'Hmm . . . why do you say that?'

'Well, don't you feel the breeze?'

'Yes, but I thought it was probably coming from the hatch behind us.'

Jimmy grinned.

'Trust me; it isn't.'

Five

'Where are you going?' Dwellings exclaimed, almost dropping his drink on the bar top.

The innkeeper turned round, slowly.

'Eh?'

'I ... um ... I'd like another drink, please,' the detective managed, sweat beading on his brow.

The innkeeper folded his arms.

'You ain't finished the one you got,' he snapped, nodding at the ale in Dwellings' hand.

'Yes, but I will shortly ... so can I have another one standing by?'

The innkeeper muttered something under his breath

and lumbered back to the bar, where he pulled Dwellings another ale.

'Satisfied?'

'Yes, thank you.'

'And you?' he asked, glaring at Wheredad.

'Oh yes. Quite satisfied, thank you.'

'Good.'

The big man turned, and headed towards the door he'd been making for earlier.

'Um . . .'

He spun around, but the movement was quicker this time . . . and he had a very disgruntled look on his face.

'WHAT NOW?'

Dwellings glanced briefly at Wheredad, thought for a moment and then said: 'How much, please?'

'You what?'

'How much for the ales?'

'You can pay when you've finished drinkin' . . .'

He turned once again, but didn't get more than a few centimetres this time.

'But we *have* finished.'

'What you on about?' the innkeeper growled, spitting on the floor as he headed back to the duo. 'He's got half a tankard left and you've got a full tankard and one waitin'. What exac'ly you tryin' to pull here, fella?'

'Trying to pull?' Dwellings gave the man a blank expression. 'We're not trying to pull anything; we're just trying to have a nice, quiet drink in the country.'

'Yeah, well, why don't you jus' shut the hell up an' get on with it, then?'

'That's not very hospitable,' Dwellings retorted, pushing his luck to see how far it would take him.

'No,' Wheredad agreed, ignoring his master's gesture to keep out of the argument. 'We could report you to the owner.'

The innkeeper stopped dead, and a terrible scowl took over his face.

'What do you know about the owner?' he asked accusingly, and Dwellings noticed that he was beginning to edge around the bar towards them.

The detective took a step back and held up his hand.

'My friend was merely pointing out that manners cost nothing,' he said. 'I assure you, we have absolutely no intention of complaining to the . . . er . . . proprietor of your establishment.'

'You couldn't anyway,' said the innkeeper, suddenly rushing to the door and throwing the bolt across it. He turned with a terrible smile on his lips. 'Owner's lyin' in the basement with 'is throat cut.'

Dwellings emptied the contents of his tankard on to the floor and waved it threateningly in the air.

'Interesting,' he said, cautiously approaching the brute as Wheredad picked up a heavy bar stool and bumbled up alongside him. 'Have you got Viscount Curfew down there, too?'

The innkeeper's face became a mask of horror.

'Spoin!' he screamed, drawing a long dagger from his apron. 'Davenpaw! Rhark! We got big trouble up here, boys!'

The innkeeper's booming voice echoed through the inn.

'Back!' Jimmy warned, hurrying into a dark corner of the cellar and hunkering down in the shadows.

Obegarde folded his black coat about him and dropped to the floor, just as the tapestry flew aside to admit two rushing figures. Obegarde immediately recognised one as the shapeshifter from the cellar; the other was a giant of a man with broad shoulders and a thick mane of hair. They hurried past, flung open the cellar's only door and took the stairs beyond it two at a time.

Jimmy sneaked up to where Obegarde was crouched.

'I knew Dwellings would blow it,' he whispered. 'Do you think we should go up and help?'

'Probably,' Obegarde admitted. 'But we've got problems of our own to deal with . . .'

'What?'

'There's somebody else coming up the tunnel . . .'

Jimmy and Obegarde stayed hidden in their dark corner as an arm brushed the tapestry aside and stepped into the sewer. The man was of medium height, slightly built and armed with a long, thin sword which he carried in a way that made both Jimmy and the vampire feel distinctly uneasy. He made straight for the door to the stairs, but before he could reach it, Obegarde steeled himself and rushed forwards . . .

'Here, have a drink!'

Enoch Dwellings swung out with the other tankard, but his arm was blocked in mid-arc by the innkeeper, who then fastened a thick hand around his neck and lifted him bodily from the ground.

'Whereg-gad! Hlp me!' he managed, struggling for breath.

Wheredad crossed the room in two leaps and smashed his bar stool across the innkeeper's back, causing the man to stagger and drop his victim. Enraged by the assault, the innkeeper spun around to land a blow of his own, but Wheredad caught him squarely on the jaw and knocked him over a table stacked with empty tankards.

'Good man, Wheredad! Jolly well do—'

Dwellings' words died in the air as the door at the back of the bar flew open and two men burst into the room.

The larger of the two leaped into the air, and a strange glow encircled his body. When he landed, he had changed into the biggest lion Dwellings had ever seen in his life. He stood, transfixed, as the beast advanced on him. There was no sign of the second man, who'd dropped behind the bar and disappeared.

Wheredad took one look at the prowling lion and

quickly made for the door, wrenching at the bar with all his might and flinging the portal wide.

'C'mon, Enoch! Get out!'

Wheredad dashed outside, but the detective wasn't with him. Glancing back, he saw that Dwellings was still standing in the centre of the inn, his gaze fixed firmly on the approaching lion.

'Enoch! ENOCH!'

From their vantage point at the edge of the wood, Lusa and Daily watched in horror as the detective's assistant rushed from the inn, screaming his master's name.

'They need help!' she said, rolling up her sleeves.

'Nah, they'll be all right,' said Daily, scratching his earlobe. 'They're a tough bunch, that lot.'

'Wheredad is screaming!'

Parsnip shrugged.

'Yeah, well, he's probably just excited.'

'I'm going in.'

'Are you? Brave girl.'

Lusa rolled her eyes, and looked around for a weapon. Unfortunately there was nothing but trees in every direction, so she grabbed a hefty branch instead, and ran for the inn . . .

. . . where Dwellings had finally snapped out of his reverie and was beginning to back away; fast.

Wheredad, who'd never been great at thinking on his feet, snatched up a fistful of stones from the road and bombed back into the inn. Ducking under a low beam, he leaped on to the table nearest the door and hailed his missiles down upon the lion, which roared with unspeakable fury at the assault.

Meanwhile, Dwellings had reached the front of the inn and was inching very carefully towards the entrance. He didn't notice the snake that was winding its way across the floor towards him.

Six

Obegarde flew into the swordsman and the two of them cannoned through the door and on to the stairs. Seizing the opportunity this afforded, Jimmy ran for the tapestry, pushed it aside and squeezed himself into the gap beyond, just as Obegarde's prey kicked him off.

Jimmy cupped a hand over his eyes, squinted.

The tunnel beyond was flickering with intermittent torchlight, and echoing with random screams. As tunnels went, it wasn't exactly a welcoming prospect, but, thankfully, Jimmy had seen a lot worse.

He grabbed one of the torches and crept forward.

* * *

As a half-vampire, Obergarde's superior strength gave him the edge over most normal men, but he was having extreme difficulty getting close to the swordfighter, who moved across the room like an eel and dodged blows like a mongoose.

Summoning a colossal burst of energy, he took a run up and leaped into the air, claws elongating in mid-flight.

Rhark slipped aside as if he was dodging a bull, and watched with amusement as Obegarde collided with the cellar wall.

'A pity, loftwing,' he said, readying his sword. 'Good run-up; poor landing.'

He darted forward and slashed Obegarde across the face with his blade. The vampire made an attempt to fight back, but the swordsman had cut him three times before he could even raise a hand.

'Interesting,' he said, stepping back to admire his handiwork. 'I thought loftwings were supposed to have lightning reflexes.'

'Oh no,' said Obegarde, using the wall to keep himself on his feet. 'That's a common misconception; we're actually quite slow. Of course, we can't be killed either, so it all evens out.'

Rhark smiled.

'Hmm . . . can't be killed, eh? It'll be fun to put that to the test, won't it?'

He drove the sword forward; it sliced through Obegarde's chest and the vampire fell to his knees.

The Dwellings Debacle

Lusa arrived at the inn just as Dwellings emerged from the door with a giant snake wrapped around him. The thing was so large that it actually covered most of his body, and Lusa could only tell that it was Dwellings from the man's atrocious choice of shoes. She jumped back, too horrified to move, but her mind was working frantically.

Fire, she thought, *we need fire.*

As Dwellings staggered around with the constricting mass engulfing him, Lusa looked down at the branch in her hand . . . and a thought struck her. She hurried towards the door of the inn, just as Wheredad flew out, backwards, underneath the biggest lion she had ever seen. The beast had already ripped a bloody chunk from Wheredad's shoulder, and was greedily snapping at his neck despite the flurry of powerful blows the big man was managing to muster.

Lusa glanced from Dwellings to Wheredad and back again. She didn't have *time* to help them both. Nevertheless, she moved fast; darting through the door of the inn and quickly scouring the room for a torch or a tinderbox. Instead, she found a lantern hanging above the bar and a handful of oil-soaked rags behind it. Counting every second, she set to work, wrapping the rags around the branch and using the lantern to tease a considerable flame from it. This done, she hurried outside and drove the makeshift torch into the lion's

face, forcing it to retreat a little way and enabling
Wheredad to scramble back across the gravel path.
Spinning around, she then hurried across the path and
lunged at the snake around Dwellings' neck.

The creature let out several long spits and started a
hissing fit. Then it released its grip on the detective and
began to retreat, sliding stealthily through the grass.
Lusa bore down on it like a crossbow bolt, stamping a
foot on to the tail of the reptile and flinging the burning
torch at its head.

The snake let out another lengthy hiss, and began
very slowly to change shape . . .

From his vantage point a good distance away, Daily
cursed himself for his cowardice: the lion had leaped
atop Wheredad once again, and if he didn't lend a hand
right now, the detective's big friend would be history . . .

Daily swore under his breath, then began hunting
around the base of the tree for a good-sized rock.

Being a rogue *and* an eternal optimist, Jimmy held out
secret hopes not only that Viscount Curfew was alive
and well, but that he'd find the noble, rescue him and
be proclaimed the ultimate hero of the hour. He didn't
expect it to be quite so easy, though.

'Lord Curfew?' he gasped, stepping back in the
corridor and holding the torch aloft. 'Is that you?'

There was a pause, then the viscount spoke.

'Yes, yes it is. Who are you?'

'Jimmy Quickstint, Lordship. We've met a few times, remember? I'm one of your loyal citizens.'

'Oh, yes . . . Jimmy. Er . . . I thank the gods you found me!'

Jimmy nodded, and moved forward to see if the viscount was wounded.

'How did you escape, Lordship? Didn't they tie you up?'

The viscount appeared to think for a moment, and then rubbed his wrists as if they'd been on fire.

'I managed to wriggle free, Johnny.'

'Jimmy, Lordship. It's *Jimmy*.'

'Yes yes, of course. I'm in a lot of pain, you understand.'

Jimmy whistled between his teeth.

'Did they torture you?'

'Indeed they did. Several times, in fact; with . . . er . . . cheese wire.'

'Oh, the devils! Never mind, Lordship, the rescue party's arrived.'

The viscount nodded.

'How did you find me?'

'I'll tell you later, Lordship.'

'No; tell me NOW.'

'No time, Lordship: really. The important thing is that we're HERE!'

'You are indeed,' said the viscount, 'and I'm *very* grateful for it; how many of you are there, exactly?'

'Er . . . five of us, sir.'

The viscount's expression changed from one of concern to one of glee.

'Oh, is that *all*? Ha! In that case, I don't know why I'm bothering with this charade . . .'

He drew a sword with lightning speed and drove it into Jimmy's stomach. The gravedigger looked down, aghast at the strike, before dropping on to the floor like a bag of potatoes.

'No hard feelings, you understand,' said the royal impostor, peering down at Jimmy with mock sympathy. 'But sometimes, people just don't want to *be* rescued.'

He stepped over the prone figure and headed up the corridor.

Spoin, the shapeshifter, was trying desperately not to change back into human form. He concentrated with all his might, but the burns on his skin were becoming more painful, and he was losing the will to sssstay a snake . . .

Lusa, horrified at the sight of the half-man, half-reptile writhing on the grass before her, summoned all of her courage. Then she hurried forward, snatched the burning torch from the ground and waved it threateningly in the creature's face.

Spoin recoiled, his forked tongue darting between his lips.

A couple of metres away, Enoch Dwellings was

attending to Wheredad, who'd managed to wriggle out from beneath the giant paws of the lion when Daily had arrived with a well-aimed rock, and was now on his knees, blood pouring from a terrible wound in his shoulder.

The lion, meanwhile, had turned his attention to the tracker and pursued him to the edge of the wood, where Daily was climbing an ancient oak tree like a spider monkey.

To make matters worse for the rescue party, night was beginning to fall across the land . . .

'Jimmy! Jimmy Quickstint; can you hear me?'

The gravedigger tried to see through the tears in his eyes, but he could only make out vague shadows.

'Help!' he cried. 'I've been stabbed; somebody help me!'

'I *will* help you,' said the voice from the end of the corridor. 'But you have to get me out of this cell; I can't do much from in here, can I?'

Jimmy made a gargantuan effort to lift his head.

'Who – who are you?' he managed, between sobs.

'Lord Curfew, of Dullitch,' said the imprisoned viscount. 'I believe we met during the Yowler incident . . .'

'We've m-met since then!' Jimmy screamed down the corridor.

'We have?'

'Yeah – you stabbed me in the stomach about six minutes ago!'

'Not me,' Curfew shouted through the bars of his prison. 'An impostor; one who will not rest until he has the entire capital crushed in his palm.'

Jimmy groaned from the pain of his wound, curled up in a tight ball.

'Can you make it over here?' Curfew called, hope creeping into his voice. 'There's a bar on the outside of the door that slides into the wall; if you can reach it and get me out, I'm sure I can help you.'

Jimmy pushed his head away from the floor once more, but the cell and its talking occupant suddenly seemed a very long way away . . .

The lion was roaring and clawing at the base of the oak like a thing possessed. Daily reached the uppermost branches of the tree and then realised that although he himself was safe, his position rendered him totally useless to the group. Oh well, he reflected, at least he could use his voice.

'HELP!' came the cry that echoed through the treetops. 'SOMEBODY HELP US! HEEELLLLLPPPP!'

$\mathcal{S}$eⱯen

'I can't kill this vampire,' Rhark said rather matter-of-factly, when his master emerged from the tapestry and joined him in the cellar. 'It's most vexing.'

'Loftwings are immortal,' the impostor said, pointing out the vampire's single fang, 'which makes them tedious company and very difficult creatures to dispose of.' He wiped some blood from his own blade with a rag and cast a glance at the pinned loftwing. 'If I were you, I really wouldn't bother.'

Rhark nodded, drew out his sword and watched Obegarde fold up like an old deck chair.

'There are more of them upstairs, master,' he said, a worried frown developing on his forehead. 'What are we going to do? Where did they all come from?'

'Dullitch,' snapped the impostor, icily. 'You must have been followed back from the city.'

'We can't have been: I checked!'

'Did you dispose of the banshee?'

'Yes, master! I dropped it in a rubbish bin on my way out of the city!'

'What about the two travellers who saw Curfew being brought in the other night?'

Rhark nodded.

'The ones Kneath killed?'

'You disposed of *them*?'

'Yes, master: just like you said to do! We took them to Dullitch and left them on a vegetable cart!'

'And you weren't seen?'

'No!'

'Did you remove their clothes?'

'What? Well, er, no, not exactly . . .'

The impostor let out a pained breath and bunched his fist.

'You fool! That would have led them to this part of Illmoor!'

'B-but it wouldn't have led them to *this* wood, master. It wouldn't have led them to *this very inn*!'

'You covered your tracks, of course?'

Rhark looked suddenly terrified. 'N-no, master. Should I have done?'

'Yes,' said the impostor, looking distractedly at his

fingernails. 'It would be fair to say that you should have done. It would be even fairer to say that you have probably led the Dullitch infantry to our very door. It's a good job you're valuable as a hired sword, my friend; if you weren't you'd be floating face-down in the sea by now . . .'

'I-I'm sorry, master; really I am! What should we do?'

'We should leave, Rhark . . . and very quickly, too.'

The sword master nodded.

'What about the others?' he hazarded.

'Oh, I wouldn't worry unduly about them; Spoin and Davenpaw are natural predators . . . and Kneath can take care of himself. *You* follow me; but stay put at the rear of the inn . . . watch my back. If I'm followed, you *deal with it*. Understand?'

'Yes, master.'

'Very good. We'll go out the back way; and do ignore the lout lying in the next corridor. I've shown him a very good trick with a blade that he's yet to recover from.'

Rhark nodded, and followed his master beyond the tapestry.

In the shadows, Obegarde rose shakily to his feet, concentrated his mind, and watched as his chest healed up.

'Curfew,' he muttered to himself. 'He can't be the villain here, surely? Why on Illmoor would a man like Curfew kidnap himself?'

Determined to find out, he bunched up both fists and headed for the secret corridor.

As footsteps hurried past him without stopping, Jimmy Quickstint struggled to his feet, staggered a little way down the corridor and promptly collapsed once again. There he lay, in the darkness, surrounded by miniature pools of his own blood, contemplating his wasted life.

'Try to make it, Jimmy!' Viscount Curfew called from the confines of his cell. 'You can do it, man!'

Jimmy groaned as a new stab of pain wracked his body. He was just considering the thought of abandoning the viscount completely when a heavily muscled arm scooped him off the ground and propped him against the brickwork.

'You've been stabbed,' said Obegarde, a concerned look on his face.

'You reckon?' Jimmy managed, forcing open one bloodshot eye. 'What gave it away, the wound itself or THE RIVER OF BLOOD YOU JUST FISHED ME OUT OF?'

'All right, all right,' the vampire muttered, ripping some material from the arm of his coat and tying it rather uselessly around the gravedigger's midriff.

'Don't let me die, Obegarde,' Jimmy pleaded. 'I'm too young . . . I haven't d-done enough stuff.'

The vampire took a closer look at the wound.

'I think you might just make it,' he said.

'B-but the blood – so much blood . . .'

'Yeah,' the vampire muttered. 'But I don't think much of this is yours – I reckon they've killed a fair few poor unfortunates down here.'

Still, he scooped Jimmy's semi-limp body into his arms and started to head back to the cellar.

'Um . . . excuse me,' called a voice. 'Do you think that when you've taken young Jimmy to get some help, you might find a quick moment to let me out of this cell, only I've been here for quite a while now and I am supposed to be running a city . . .'

Obegarde recognised the voice and spun around.

'Lord Curfew!' he boomed. 'Is that you? I mean, is that *really* you?'

'Yes, damn it! And the evil cretins who kidnapped me are getting away, so if you've not got the wherewithal to stop them, then at least GET ME OUT OF THIS DAMN PRISON so that I can!'

Obegarde knelt down, and deposited the moaning rogue gently on the cold stones. Then he shouted: 'Get back, Viscount!' and took a run up at the cell door.

There was an incredibly loud crash, and Obegarde slid down the portal like a pancake thrown at a wall.

Curfew's face reappeared at the door-hatch.

'Erm . . . I actually just wanted you to slide the bolt back,' he said.

'Ghrfff,' said Obegarde, peeling his nose from the stone. Then, clawing on to wall nooks for purchase, he dragged himself to his feet and snatched at the bolt.

The door flew open, and Curfew marched determinedly into the corridor, dabbing some blood from a cut above his lip.

'Right,' he said, snatching a curved sword from a display hook on the wall next to the cell. '*Now* you can get your friend to safety: *I've* got some vengeance to wreak.'

Eight

'HELP! SOMEBODY HELP US!'

'There!' Burnie cried, slapping his steed on the flank. The horse reared up and bolted through the wood in the direction of the shouts, its companions soon urged to follow suit.

Seconds later, all eleven riders erupted through the fringe of the wood like a wall of thunder.

Spires quickly surveyed the scene, but the little troglodyte was some way ahead of him.

'The lion!' he screamed. 'I want two men on the lion! And somebody help that injured bloke . . . and the girl with the snake-man!'

Several guards dismounted and dashed around

the clearing like headless chickens, screaming the
Dullitch war cry and frantically waving their
swords. The remaining squadron descended on
the lion like the wrath of gods, driving swords at the
beast and forcing it to retreat into the heart of the
wood.

Kneath came bolting out of the inn brandishing a
chair-leg, only to be mercilessly cut down before he
reached Enoch Dwellings, who was helping a guard lift
Wheredad on to one of the horses.

The writhing form of Spoin curled back as the guards
advanced, their swords waved threateningly in front of
them.

'Kill it!' Burnie screamed at them. 'It's evil; they all
are! And you three: don't let that lion get away!'

There were a few dog-eared salutes as several
men galloped into the woods beyond, but the guards
gathered around the snake were simply too slow to
catch it.

Burnie swallowed, and shook his head at the overall
scene. Then he turned to get Spires' opinion on the
proceedings, but the secretary was gone . . .

Spires had dismounted from his steed and was dashing
towards the back of the inn. A few minutes earlier,
while peering through the spyglass, he'd seen
something he couldn't quite bring himself to believe.
Viscount Curfew had emerged from the rear of the

building, followed by ... Viscount Curfew. The two men, one of whom was undoubtedly his master, looked completely identical.

He'd given chase immediately, but had lost them when they entered the wood. Still, the important thing was that they *both* had seen him coming, so the viscount would know that help was at hand ...

He quickened his pace, hurrying towards the edge of the wood as fast as he was able. Behind him, in the shadows cast by the inn's dark face, Rhark detached himself from the back wall, took a sizeable run-up and cannoned into the royal secretary, knocking him straight to the ground.

'Greetings, pathetic grovel-hog of spineless nobles,' he spat, leaping up and kicking the secretary hard in the stomach. 'I am Rhark, sword master extraordinaire. Happy to meet you.'

He dragged Spires up by his collar and threw a punch, but the secretary blocked it and caught him with a well-placed knee in the privates.

'Ash!'

As the sword master doubled up in agony, Spires shoved him aside and bolted into the woods, unwittingly losing his sword in the process.

'You better run, little man!' Rhark screamed at the clustered trees. 'You better run good and fast!'

Darkness gathered over the land. Night was fast approaching ... and the wind had a bite to it.

* * *

The unconscious form of Jimmy Quickstint cradled firmly in his arms, Obegarde kicked open the remains of the Lostings front door and emerged on to a scene of absolute mayhem.

A large man in an apron, presumably the innkeeper, had been wounded by the guards and was currently being read his rights by the unmistakable troglodyte who ran the Dullitch Council.

There were more guards emerging from the nearby woods, dragging the enormous, hairy body of a man behind them.

Obegarde smiled when he saw Lusa running towards him, waving her arms.

'Father!'

The vampire smiled.

'I'm OK, sweetheart! What are these guards doing he—'

'Father! LOOK OUT!'

Obegarde spun around just in time to see the snake-man – in human form, aside from his reptilian head – leap into the air.

Having learned a valuable lesson in his struggle with Rhark, the vampire moved with near lightning speed, dropping Jimmy on the ground so hard that the gravedigger almost bounced. Rising up, he brought the snake-man out of the air with a body tackle, and sank his elongated fang deep into Spoin's scale-covered neck.

The creature gave a terrible cry and began to convulse with shock.

In seconds, the guards were on them, some slashing at the creature while others helped Obegarde to detach himself from it. One even bent down to see how Jimmy was doing, and quickly called back for a first-aid kit.

'Thank the gods you're all right,' Lusa said breathlessly, dropping on to her knees as she neared the vampire. 'I didn't realise . . . well, what I mean is, I didn't think . . .'

'I could take him?' Obegarde ventured. 'Mmm . . . you've got a lot to learn about your old dad yet . . . and, I warn you – none of it's good.'

Lusa smiled, but somewhat vaguely.

'Do you mind if we go home now? Only, I've left Tiddles in the basement and I'm really quite worried about him.'

'Well, I'm sure he'll be fine; he's a very resourceful cat.'

'Am I alive?' said a strangled voice, causing both Obegarde and Lusa to start.

Jimmy Quickstint forced open a leaky eyelid.

'No,' Obegarde replied, leaning over the gravedigger with an evil smile. 'This is the afterlife, and I'm your companion. You've been condemned to hell for a lifetime of pilfering and bad decisions.'

Jimmy's eyelid flickered, and a tear began to form.

'B-but I helped save Dullitch . . . twice!'

'I know,' Obegarde said, mockingly. '*They* were the
bad decisions.'

Lusa broke first; and suffered a sudden fit of giggles.
'Shhh! Stop it! He'll hear you!'

'Oi! I know that voice! Obegarde . . . is that you?'

'Of course it is, you numbskull.'

The gravedigger sat up.

'I'm not dead, then!' he cried, relief flooding over
him. 'How can that be? I was stabbed in the stomach!'

'No,' Obegarde corrected. 'You were stabbed in this
. . .'

The vampire reached out with thumb and forefinger
and plucked up the skewered body of Kyn Blistering's
hamster.

'Wow!' Jimmy exclaimed. 'Y'see? I told you it was
magical!'

Obegarde smiled wanly, and wondered just how many
gods were looking out for Jimmy Quickstint.

'He all right?' said Burnie, carefully dismounting from
his horse.

'He'll be fine,' said the vampire, seriously. 'But if I
were you, I'd get after Viscount Curfew: the enemy is a
man who looks exactly like him . . . and once they're
together, we'll have no hope of telling them apart.'

'Identical, you say?'

'*Absolutely* identical.'

Burnie clambered back on to his horse, and snatched
up the reins.

'I'll go myself,' he said, checking his belt dagger. 'Save your concern, though: only the royal bloodline can wear the Seal Ring. No impostor can or will ever sit on the Dullitch throne.'

With that, he urged his horse into a gallop and hared off in the direction of the wood.

Nine

Spires dashed through the gloomy wood, leaping bushes and swiping branches from his path in a desperate attempt to reach Lord Curfew before the sword master reached *him*. He had no fear for his own safety, but his primary mission was the same as it had always been: to serve and protect the Lord of Dullitch . . . at any cost.

Spires darted left and right, urgently scanning the woods for any sign of the two. Unfortunately, before he had time to focus on the glades dotted all around him, he was leaped upon and forced to the ground.

Rhark somersaulted forward and hurtled on to his feet, drawing his sword in the process.

'Get up,' he yelled at the secretary, swinging the sword as he circled the glade. 'Foolish servant of cowards, get up and fight for your survival.'

Spires staggered to his feet and reached for his own sword, but the sheath was empty.

'Lost it, have you?' Rhark tormented. 'Mislaid your only weapon in the woods? Pathetic incompetents such as yourself *deserve* no mercy, but worry not – you shall die in the manner befitting a fool . . .'

He drew a long dagger from his belt pouch with a free hand, and pitched it with unerring precision at the secretary's leg.

Spires cried out as the blade bit into him, and collapsed into a crumpled heap upon the forest floor.

'P-please . . .'

'Ahh,' Rhark chided. 'Here comes the begging; my favourite part.'

Spires held up a shaking hand.

'C-come no closer, enemy of Dullitch . . .'

'Hahaha! Enemy of Dullitch; how quaint! Now, I think, is the time to end this little pantomime. The question is, how. Hmm . . . a beheading, perhaps?'

Rhark raised his sword at a wide angle, and ran at the secretary. At the last moment, he leaped into the air and swung back the sword . . .

And Spires shot him straight in the face.

* * *

Swords clashed, glanced each other and clashed again.

Viscount Curfew stepped back, keeping his eyes firmly on the feet of the impostor.

'You can't win, you know . . .' said the mock viscount. 'I don't doubt you'll put up a brave fight, but in the end, you'll be destroyed.'

'Thankfully,' Curfew snarled back, 'overconfidence isn't your only weakness.'

'That's right,' said the impostor, performing a near perfect lunge of his own. 'I'm also far too merciful.'

Curfew blocked the strike, but only just.

He lunged forward with his sword, but the move was quickly parried by the impostor.

'Is that the best you've got, *my lord*? Ha! No wonder you were easy pickings for Rhark.'

The scream echoed through the wood.

Rhark landed on his feet, clutched frantically at his face, and staggered forward.

Spires pulled himself up and took several steps back, then he produced a mini-crossbow from his belt hook and aimed it at the flailing sword master's chest.

'A bolt in the heart, perhaps?' he said mockingly, and squeezed the trigger.

There was a quick *swwwwck*, one final scream and a dull thud, and Rhark, sword master extraordinaire, fell silent.

* * *

'What was that?' the impostor demanded, circling his opponent with the air of the suddenly preoccupied.

Viscount Curfew licked his lips.

'My cavalry has arrived,' he said. 'They might take their time, but they strike with a vengeance once angered.'

To underline the observation, Curfew ran a single finger along his throat. 'I'm no voice expert, but that scream sounded like your man with the swords.'

'Never,' the impostor snapped, swinging his sword in a rough circle. 'When it comes to steel, Rhark cannot be bested.'

'So you say,' muttered Curfew. 'But my secretary is a very resourceful man. He, too, is difficult to match.'

'Ha! I think not, *my lord*. Your secretary, from what I've heard tell, is a bumbling, twitching, disconsolate fool, much like yourself.'

'Really? Then I should back up your words with steel.'

Curfew dived forward and drove his sword at the impostor's neck. The shade parried, dropped to his knees and slashed at Curfew's mid-section, a move that the viscount evaded by the narrowest of margins.

'You fight surprisingly well for a *reflection*. Perhaps, as one of us is going to die here anyway, you will tell me your true identity?'

The impostor blocked another of Curfew's lunges, and shook his head.

'That knowledge will never be yours, *my lord*. Never.'

'Such secrecy,' the viscount remarked, switching his sword from one hand to the other. 'Must be a hideously ugly countenance you're hiding in there.'

'You have no idea,' said the impostor, his voice suddenly edged with emotion. 'You have absolutely no idea.'

He lunged again, but with renewed vigour . . . and almost caught Curfew off balance.

'You know nothing about the time that I have waited, and the *suffering* that I have endured.'

'Granted,' replied the viscount. 'But it'll be nothing compared to the suffering you'll endure if you don't put down that sword and surrender yourself to me.'

'Why don't you both put down your swords?'

The two viscounts turned to regard the staggering form of Spires, who entered the clearing with a black look on his face and the miniature crossbow raised.

'What do you mean, "both"?' said Curfew, outraged. 'It's me, Spires!'

The secretary nodded.

'I know you're there somewhere, Excellency,' he managed. 'It's just a matter of finding out which one is the real you.'

'You can't be serious, man! 'said the viscount. 'Use your mind, not your eyes! I know he's wearing the Seal Ring, but . . .'

'He IS wearing it! Then *you're* the impostor!'

'No, listen to me! He's found some way to counter its power. It's ME, Spires.'

The impostor tried to hide his smile, but it faded naturally when the secretary fished in his pocket, and produced the second of the city's Seal Rings.

'Lucky I brought this along: put this on.'

He tossed the ring across to Curfew, who caught it gratefully and obliged.

Nothing happened.

'You see, it *is* me!' the viscount pleaded. 'This proves it!'

'No,' Spires muttered. 'It only proves that the villain has found a way to counter it.'

'But it's ME, Spires: don't you recognise my voice?'

'Of course I do; you both sound the same. Now, drop your swords, please: I need to think . . .'

Curfew shook his head.

'A noble never relinquishes his weapon, Spires.'

'Never,' added the copy. 'And well you should know it, man!'

Spires glanced from one to the other, a confused look on his face.

'Your weapons,' he said, in conclusion. 'And I shan't ask again.'

Curfew looked deep into the secretary's craggy face, and relinquished his weapon. The impostor followed suit, so quickly, in fact, that both swords bit into the dirt at the same time.

'Good,' said Spires, careful to keep his crossbow aimed as he collected both weapons. 'Now move over to the

big tree behind you: we're going to have a little question and answer session . . . and a wrong answer is likely to leave one of you *wanting*.'

'Did you hear the news?' Lusa said, hurrying over to where Dwellings stood, untying his horse. 'Obegarde says that the kidnapping was masterminded by a man who looks identical to Viscount Curfew. Mr Spires and the troglodyte are looking for them now . . . what if they get the wrong one?'

'Fret none,' Dwellings smiled. 'There are certain *magics* protecting the viscount's bloodline.'

'Like the ring?'

'Like the ring.'

Lusa nodded.

'So what will you do now?' she said.

'Nothing,' said Dwellings, proudly, mounting his horse

and waiting for Lusa to climb up behind him. 'I solved the case. I may have had help from Wheredad, Daily, Obegarde and yourself, but I – Enoch Dwellings – worked out the essentials! Don't you realise what this means, and how monumental it is? I'm actually living up to my name as the Greatest Detective in the History of Dullitch!'

'Mmm,' Lusa replied, rather unenthusiastically. 'Did you come up with that all by yourself?'

'Yes,' Dwellings snapped, rounding on the girl with furrowed brows. 'Why, what's wrong with it?'

'Well, nothing really,' she said, climbing up behind him. 'It's just a bit, er, pompous, isn't it?'

'Pompous? Pompous!'

'Yes.'

'Well, I'll have you know that a lot of women find "pompous" men very attractive!'

'Do they?' Lusa looked suitably surprised. 'Goodness; how odd.' She peered across the clearing, to the horse that carried one of the viscount's soldiers and the wounded Wheredad. 'Do you think he'll be all right?' she asked, trying to sound casual. 'He was ever so brave back there, fighting that lion . . .'

'Oh, he'll be fine,' Dwellings muttered. 'More's the pity.'

'What was that?'

'Nothing, I was just thinking out loud.'

'Oh.'

'He's never had a girlfriend, you know . . .'

Lusa looked up, suddenly.

'I'm sorry?'

'Wheredad; he's never had a girlfriend in his life!'

'Really?' Lusa smiled over at the detective's half-conscious assistant. 'That's so sweet.'

Enoch Dwellings, the Greatest Detective in the History of Dullitch, swore under his breath, cursed the gods, and urged his horse into a tired trot. Some girls, he felt certain, just weren't worth the effort.

'Listen to me very carefully,' said Spires, eyeing the identical lords with suspicion. 'I'll ask you each a question and I don't want you answering for each other; understood?'

Two nods, two confident smiles.

'Question one,' Spires continued, raising the crossbow and pointing it at the impostor. 'What is my middle name?'

'How should I know?' came the answer. 'I never discuss personal issues with the staff.'

Spires gasped.

'B-but I've worked in your service for *years*!' he said, breathlessly. 'You must be the impostor.' He quickly turned the crossbow on Curfew. 'Tell him the right answer, Excellency!'

The viscount tugged at the lobe of his ear.

'Is it Rupert?' he hazarded, to the apparent horror of
his secretary.

'I don't believe this!' Spires snapped, glaring at both
men with disappointment in his eyes. 'I'm your most
important servant; how can you not know my middle
name?'

Two impassive shrugs.

Spires gritted his teeth, and fought on.

'OK, then. By what name did the contessa call you when
you came home two days late from the Legrash Carnival?'

'How am I supposed to answer that?' Curfew snapped.
'You know my memory's appalling!'

'Yes,' the impostor agreed. 'He might be a fake, but
he's got a valid point, there: our memory *is* atrocious.'

Spires held the crossbow level, and racked his brains
for a solution.

'I've got one,' he said, eventually. 'And it's something
that every Lord of Dullitch knows like the back of his
hand.'

'Go on,' said the two men, in unison.

'Why did Duke Vitkins defend a downed harpy from
his own citizens when Dullitch was under attack from
the Undead Horde?'

'I don't remember,' said Viscount Curfew, whose
father had so repeatedly drummed the story into him as
a child that he'd deliberately blocked it from his mind
at an early age. 'I'm sorry, Spires, but I really, honestly
don't remember.'

'She was his daughter,' said the impostor.

Spires stared from one to the other with a shocked, almost ghostlike look on his face.

'What did you say?' he muttered, trying to decide whether or not his master could have forgotten such an important fact.

'The harpy was Vitkins' daughter,' the impostor repeated. 'She was converted to the forces of darkness by Liss, then Arch-lord of the Zombies, and mutated beyond recognition; to all but her father, that is.'

Spires nodded.

'That is the correct answer,' he said, swallowing. 'I can't believe that any true Lord of Dullitch would be ignorant of that tale. Step over to me, please, Excellency.'

'Spires! No!'

Curfew made to step forward, but the secretary shot him in the arm.

'Arghhhh!'

'Good man, Spires,' said the impostor, hurrying across the clearing while the secretary fought to reload his weapon. 'Let me just grab these swords, and we can do away with this . . . *enchanted wretch.*'

He reached down and snatched up both swords as Curfew struggled to stay upright, then he moved to stand behind the secretary, with a wicked smile on his face.

'I'm sorry, whoever you are,' Spires said, eyeing

Curfew with a mixture of disgust and pity. 'But no one imitates the Lord of Dullitch without getting their comeuppance.'

'I'm sorry too,' said Curfew, shaking his head. 'Sorry for you, *old friend.*'

A flash of recognition suddenly dawned in the secretary's watery eyes, and he spun around with the crossbow readied . . .

. . . but the impostor's sword found its mark first.

Spires let out a blood-curdling scream . . . and fell at the feet of his master's doppelganger.

'Interesting,' said the impostor, studying the sword-edge. 'These blades really are quite sharp, aren't they? Here, take this.' He tossed the other sword across to Curfew. 'After all, *my lord*, I'd hate to be accused of anything but fair play . . .'

Curfew wiped away tears of frustration as he snatched up the proffered weapon and staggered across the clearing, trying to block out the searing pain in his leg.

'Come now, *my lord*, I'm sure he didn't feel much pain. I mean, look at his face; he *is* smiling . . .'

Curfew lunged forward, almost catching the impostor off guard. The swords clashed viciously; once, twice, then Curfew dropped down on to his good knee and tried for a last, desperate leg swipe. He missed, and the impostor used his own blade to block the misjudged attack. This time, as the swords met, Curfew's blade was broken in half.

Shock overcame the viscount, and his arms fell limply to his sides. The impostor swiftly sheathed his own sword and, booting Curfew squarely in the chest, drove him back, hard.

The viscount collided with a tree, but managed to swing himself aside before the impostor's fist could find its mark. Then he drove an elbow into the man's back, kicked hard at his side and, as he stumbled round, slammed a punch so hard into his face that a spray of blood erupted from his nose.

'That's for Spires,' he growled, and reached down for the impostor's sheathed sword. However, this time the man was ready: it was as if he'd been given a second wind by some unseen force of energy. His eyes glinted with evil intent as he grasped Curfew's wrist.

The viscount winced as he heard his bones snap under the pressure of the impostor's grip.

'Try to take measured breaths, *Excellency*,' the man mimicked. 'It will *prolong* your pain. Hahahaha!'

Curfew punched and kicked with all his might, but found every blow blocked with comparative ease. Eventually, when all other tactics had failed, he threw himself bodily at the fiend in a last-ditch attempt to take him down. The plan backfired: badly.

The impostor stepped aside, tripping Curfew in the process. Then he snatched up the viscount's feet and began to swing him around, faster and faster,

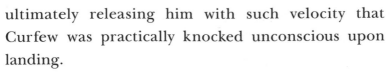

ultimately releasing him with such velocity that Curfew was practically knocked unconscious upon landing.

The impostor wiped a stream of blood from his face, and grinned down at the viscount.

'The Great Viscount Curfew, Lord and Master of Dullitch. Ha! Look at you now; beaten, broken and *far* from your throne.'

Curfew tried to stand, but the impostor glanced a boot heel off his face, flooring him once again.

The viscount coughed several times, then tried to roll over and, failing that, raised himself on to his elbows. He was now fighting for breath.

'W-w-who *are* you?'

The impostor smiled.

'Right now, I'm you,' he said. 'Beyond that, you don't need to know. Just assure yourself that I'm . . . *nobody new in your life.*'

Curfew tried to push himself up from the ground, yet still he lacked strength.

'Nobody new? What does that mean?' A sudden thought struck him. 'Duke Modeset? It can't be – is it? Is it you?'

The impostor made a face, but to Curfew's relief his sword stayed firmly in its scabbard.

'Modeset?' he said, with a cunning smile. 'Hahahaha! Now there's a name I haven't heard in a very long time. No, I'm afraid I am most definitely *not* Vandre Modeset.

However, if it comes as any sort of consolation, I *did*
know him quite well.'

'Of course you did,' Curfew muttered, finally
managing to struggle to his feet. 'And thanks for the
clue. Now I know where I know you from; the face and
voice may be mine, but the *expressions* and the laugh
remain unmistakably your own.'

'Oh?'

'Indeed . . . the funny thing is, I haven't heard such
cruelty in a laugh since I was sixteen years old, and
studying at Crestwell.'

'Oh, do tell,' said the impostor with mock interest,
drawing his sword as an afterthought.

'His name was Sorrell Diveal,' Curfew went on,
backing away from his opponent very slowly. 'Though
everyone called him Sorry. He was a nasty piece of
work in every respect, and he always had his eye set on
Dullitch. Unfortunately, he was last in line to the throne;
a fact that twisted and fractured his heart.'

'Shame,' said the impostor, now aiming his sword as
if to strike. 'What happened to him?'

Curfew, resigned to his fate, smiled at the prompt
he'd been waiting for.

'Well, he ended up throwing away his birthright.
You see, he got himself trained as a dark sorcerer in
Shinbone. Then he made the mistake of his life: he
tried to take the town. It was a bad move, it really was.
Reinforcements arrived from Crust and wiped out his

rag-tag army of trolls, imps and half-breeds. He himself disappeared, never to be seen again.'

'Hmm . . . a very sad story,' said the impostor, his grin undeterred.

'Oh, yes, it is,' Curfew agreed. 'But the thing that always made me laugh about it was, they were planning to offer him the throne of Shinbone the very next day . . .'

'SILENCE!' the impostor screamed, and bolted across the clearing, swinging out wildly with his sword. 'That's a liiiie!'

Curfew just managed to dodge the lunge, and watched as the man's sword-edge bit into the tree bark beside him.

'They would never have given me the throne!' Diveal cried. 'They would all have *died* before they saw me crowned!'

'Quite right,' said Curfew, too pained to run and too exhausted to argue. 'Hello, Sorrell; it's been a long, long time. Where exactly *have* you been hiding?'

Sorrell Diveal wrenched his blade from the tree and turned, a wicked glint in his eye.

'Hiding? No,' he muttered. 'Watching and waiting. Not to mention gathering some unique talents to my aid. Dullitch has always belonged to me, Ravis, whether by right or intention. I've seen it plagued with rats, I've seen it almost turned to stone, and I've seen it harshly neglected by two pathetic incompetents who laid no greater claim to the place than I!'

'But we *did* have greater claim, Sorrell; that's all there was to it. Don't you remember the lineage classes at school? First came Modeset, then me and finally you.'

'Ha! A dismal *third* in line . . .'

'Indeed; a damn sight better than the other lords, though, and *they* all accepted *their* own destinies, shared the smaller cities between them . . .'

'Oh yes . . . and look how they turned out! Vadney Sapp went mad, Muttknuckles managed to bankrupt Shinbone and Victor Blood filled Legrash with ghouls! I would've done a far greater job with the capital; it just wasn't fair!'

'Nothing's fair,' Curfew snapped, steeling himself for the assault to come. 'But that's the way things are; life's a bit—'

Sorrell screamed vengeance and brought his sword down, hard.

Curfew tried to move, but the blade caught him in the stomach and he fell.

'Does it hurt, Ravis?' Sorrell enquired, circling the viscount with spit flying from his twisted mouth. 'Is the pain . . . unfortunate? You're wrong, you know, life isn't a bitch, it's a joke . . . and here's the punch line.'

An ear-splitting scream echoed through the wood, and then . . . silence reigned.

Eleven

Viscount Curfew staggered to his feet and wiped the blood from his sword.

Emerging from the woods, he saw that the sun had risen high over the mountains, bathing the land in a bright new morning.

'Lord Curfew?' called a voice behind him. 'Don't move, now – it's *me*, Burnie!'

The viscount froze as the troglodyte steered his horse along the fringe of the trees, his dagger drawn at his side.

'Stay still, please, and raise your right hand. I need to make sure it is you and not the . . . other.'

The viscount turned and did as he was told, extending his right hand in front of him.

There was a pause, followed by a significant sigh of relief from the troglodyte.

'Thank the gods, Excellency! We were all so worried about you.'

He urged his horse closer to the viscount and reached out a gloopy hand.

'Are you hurt?'

Curfew shook his head.

'No, not at all; I'm just extremely tired.'

Burnie nodded, and helped his lord up into the saddle behind him.

'What about Mr Spires, Excellency? Is he OK?'

Curfew shook his head.

'Unfortunately not, my friend. He was slain by the fiend who orchestrated this whole, insane plot.'

'The impostor?'

'Yes.'

'W-where . . .'

'In the black heart of the wood; I managed to drag him along with me for a time, but we'll certainly need help in order to get both bodies safely back to the city.'

'Both bodies, Excellency? Are you sure you *want* to bring the body of that fiend back with you?'

'Absolutely; after all, he still looks like me . . . and I'm desperate to find out how he achieved such sorcery. I want to forget this dreadful business as much as you, but I must ensure that such a conspiracy never takes place again.'

'Of course, Excellency. I'll have the men find both bodies. Now, do make sure you hold on tight!'

Burnie urged his horse into a trot, then a gallop; as it neared the edge of the wood, Sorrell Diveal looked back over one shoulder, and grinned. Far in the distance, the city of Dullitch awaited . . . and with it, his throne.

He took a measured breath, and prepared himself for the ultimate deception . . .

Epilogue

The kidnap and subsequent murder of Viscount Curfew signalled a new era in the history of Dullitch, an era in which the city would find itself beguiled, besotted and betrayed by a powerful necromancer with an unshakable belief that the throne belonged rightfully to him.

Yet the thieving, throat-snatching citizens of Dullitch were used to necromancers, and the city that had seen more dukes than dustmen wasn't about to roll over and play dead for anyone . . .

Coming soon ...

The Vanquish Vendetta

DAVID LEE STONE

Viscount Curfew has been returned to Dullitch, but things
are not as they seem. The real Curfew was brutally
murdered and now an evil impostor sits on his throne.
Ruthless and hungry for power, he will do anything to
sustain his disguise ... and people have started to notice.
But this impostor is a pawn of a much darker force. One
that's older than Illmoor itself ...

Meanwhile, elsewhere ...

King Groan Teethgrit, his brother Gape, and Gordo
Goldeaxe discover an ancient and valuable hammer that
leads them back to Dullitch. Little do they know they have
just unearthed a crucial part of Dullitch's past.

Can old heroes reunite to save the city once again?

THE **illmoor**
CHRONICLES

The Ratastrophe Catastrophe

Illmoor, a country of contradiction, conflict and chicanery. A country riddled with magic, both light and dark ... and a capital city overrun with ... RATS.

The nice young man Duke Modeset hired to rid the city of its plague has run off with its children, and unless the Duke can track him down and bring the children back, he's DEAD ...

The Yowler Foul-up

A terrible sect has arisen in Illmoor. They're dark, they're deadly and they're even more hellbent on the destruction of the city than the citizens themselves. All that stand between total chaos and the return of the dark gods are Duke Modeset (who doesn't like the place anyway), Jareth Obegarde (a vampire on his mother's side) and Jimmy Quickstint (who is about to do the wrong favour for the wrong man).

A thrilling story of darkness and destiny, where the brave step forward ... and fall over.

The Shadewell Shenanigans

Groan Teethgrit and Gordo Goldeaxe have looted one village too many, and now the Lords of Illmoor are baying for their blood. Can Duke Modeset, exiled Lord of Dullitch, devise a plan clever enough to topple the duo AND Groan's equally reckless half-brother? Of course he can't, he's next to useless himself ...

... but he does have one secret weapon: an extremely beautiful princess who seems willing to do absolutely nothing for the good of her country.

www.illmoorchronicles.com